Sweeter in the Summer

OLIVIA MILES

~ Rosewood Press ~

ISBN 978-0692474778

SWEETER IN THE SUMMER

Cover design by Go On Write

First Edition: July 2015

Sweeter in the Summer

Chapter One

Lila Harris glanced at the antique cuckoo clock on the wall one last time, waiting for the little wooden door to open and the carved bluebird to appear. Tense seconds chipped away, until—Lila jumped, as she always did when the chimes went off, and laughed softly. Taking a deep breath, she slid her chair back and stood to smooth her skirt. The tote on her desk was packed and ready. Nails painted. Shoes, new.

She acknowledged her assistant's thumbs-up with a nervous smile, and pushed out the front door, her hand grazing the railing as she ran down the stairs of the building, her eyes darting for a cab. The sun was beating down on the pavement, showing promise of another warm day. Lila held a hand to shield her eyes from the sun and fixed her stare in the distance.

"Good afternoon, Lila!" called Jim Watson, whose law office was on the second floor of the Lincoln Park brownstone, just above hers. He grinned as he approached. "It's beginning to feel like summer!"

"Finally," she agreed, lifting her hand to flag a driver scouting for fares. The cabbie flashed its signal, and she felt a little skip in her pulse. "Enjoy your lunch!"

Jim held up his brown bag as he climbed the stairs to the building's front door. "You, too!"

Inside the cab, the air was thick with heat, but if she closed her eyes, Lila could almost imagine she was at the beach, with the sand in her toes and the breeze in her hair. This weekend she had a date with the lake. But today. . . She pressed her hand to her stomach. Today she was on a mission.

The cab rolled through the neighborhood, winding down sleepy residential streets where mothers pushed baby carriages and neighbors stopped to chat on the stoop, their toddlers licking melting popsicles or drawing with chalk, and eventually turned down Lake Shore Drive, where it picked up speed. Lila tried to focus on the buildings, the architecture she'd never stopped appreciating, the view of the lake, and then the river. Finally, the cab rolled to a stop, and Lila handed over a twenty, not bothering to ask for change, even though the tip was generous and a few extra bucks could go a long way right now. If she stalled, she might lose her nerve, and confidence was key.

Stepping out into the sunshine, Lila bit her lip against

the searing pain of the blister that was starting to form on her left heel, and steered her way through the sidewalk traffic. The doors to the restaurant were big. Looming and dark and far too mysterious. What was on the other side? Were they already waiting for her?

Maybe they were. That wouldn't be so bad, she told herself, shaking her shoulders back. So her knees were wobbling and her stomach was twisting so tightly she could barely breathe—they wouldn't notice. What they *would* notice was how prepared she was. How eager—*no, not eager*, she thought, as a familiar wave of nausea took over. She definitely didn't want to appear eager, even if she was.

Honestly, she was being ridiculous. She had been to dozens of meetings like this. So what if Reed Sugar was . . . There was that flutter again. There was no fighting it. A meeting with a major household brand was a very big deal.

The door handle was warm under her palm, and she knew she was pausing for an unnatural amount of time. A middle-aged man came up behind her, frowning with impatience, looking at her like she was half-crazy, and Lila blew out a breath. This was it.

"May I help you?" A smiling hostess stopped her as she entered the dimly restaurant.

"I'm meeting with Jeremy Reed," Lila explained, glancing around the lobby for a glimpse of her high school classmate. The warm lead was half the battle; the rest was up to her.

The woman checked the reservation book. "You're the first to arrive. Would you like to wait over in the bar area?"

Lila crossed the room and perched on the edge of a free chair, ready to jump up at a moment's notice. She pressed her palms firmly on her knees, feeling the slick sweat of her skin, and pushed down until her nerves had subsided.

Not wanting to look stalkerish or *eager* or anything, she trained her attention on the reservation desk, where the hostess was giggling at something a man was saying. Lila leaned in, happy for the distraction, the excuse to drown out her surroundings, and the gut-churning anticipation that grew with each second that ticked by.

The man's suit was dark and well cut, and two polished cufflinks adorned a crisp white dress shirt. The hostess said something as she reached for the phone and the man laughed. It was a deep laugh: warm, rich, and sincere. And oddly familiar.

Lila felt a twitch of panic as a disturbing thought took hold. It couldn't be. Not *him*. Okay, so his hair was brown and he was sort of the same height, and the laugh *was* familiar, but then how many men over the years had drummed up a memory she'd rather forget? Chances were he'd turn around and remind her of how silly she was being. He probably had freckles and brown eyes and— *Oh, no.*

A cold knot formed deep in her stomach and her heart

began to pound so loudly she could feel the rush in her ears. Lila looked away slowly, careful to keep her expression neutral so he might think she hadn't even seen him, and shifted in her chair, her back firmly to the bar.

God help her. It was Sam.

*

He would have recognized her anywhere.

Sam Crawford gripped the strap of his briefcase and stared at the back of Lila's head, wondering what the hell he should do, what he should say to her. If he should say anything at all. He knew that she had moved home after leaving New York, but he hadn't counted on running into her like this. He'd been to Chicago a few times since their last bitter conversation all those years ago, and he'd kept an eye out, hoping for a chance meeting, an excuse to talk, a casual reason to reconnect that didn't involve drudging up the dirty past.

Today of all days. The timing couldn't have been worse.

He turned his attention back to the hostess, forcing a grin. "I spot a friend over there, actually. If you'll just notify me when the rest of my party arrives, I'd appreciate it."

Friend was a stretch. It had been years since he and Lila had spoken, and their parting had been far from amicable. With his briefcase tight in his fist, Sam walked to the bar and ordered a scotch, the corner of his eye firmly centered on Lila. She hadn't seen him, or if she had, she was doing a damn good job of pretending she hadn't. The thought of it bothered him. More than it should.

She was still pretty, he noticed, both pleased and annoyed by his observation. If anything, she had only changed for the better over time, growing from a wide-eyed, slightly overwhelmed girl into a graceful young woman. Her oval face was pale but proud; her chestnut-colored hair was pulled back, revealing the long sweep of her neck. From the way she dressed, Sam could only assume she was waiting for a coworker or other professional acquaintance, and he felt a twinge of relief to know that she wasn't on a date.

Like it mattered.

Taking a long swig of his drink, his eyes remained fixed on her over the rim of his glass. The bar was filling quickly with the lunch crowd, and his own appointment would start at any moment. He had a decision to make and he couldn't stand here debating it much longer. He could cross the room and say hello, or he could leave the past in the past.

Lila's eyes shifted, just enough that he had to think fast, and before she could look away he held up a hand. *No going back now.* He grinned, finding it much easier than he wanted it to be. In return, Lila offered him a small, tentative smile.

Sam set his drink down and loosened his tie. She'd given him all the encouragement he needed.

*

Lila watched helplessly as Sam approached her, one hand thrust casually in his pocket, the other carrying his briefcase. His face was so familiar, but even more handsome than she'd dared to remember, as luck would have it. Time had been good to him; the six years since she'd last seen him had brought a few more lines around his eyes, but only she would have noticed. She'd memorized his face. The lift of his mouth when he smiled, the tousle of his hair when he slept . . .

"Lila Harris," Sam said quietly, offering her a friendly smile. Standing to meet him, Lila straightened her shoulders in a failed attempt to regain her composure. Her head slightly inclined, they stood face to face. Those blue eyes had always been her undoing.

"Sam." Her voice was hoarse. Awkwardly, she cleared her throat, feeling a heat rise in her cheeks as he continued to stare at her. "What a surprise." She forced a tight smile.

"A pleasant one, I hope?"

She struggled to make out his expression. Happiness? Fear? Remorse? But then, perhaps he felt nothing. Perhaps to him, she was just a thing of the past, someone he had forgotten a long time ago.

She waited for the burn to leave her face and hoped the room was dark enough that he wouldn't notice.

"What brings you to Chicago?" Lila managed. One question at a time. A few minutes of small talk. Then it would be over. Again. She could do this. "I thought you were still in New York."

"I'm in town for a meeting," Sam said mildly, his eyes never straying from hers. "I just flew in this morning."

Lila glanced at the door, happy for the excuse to look away. Still no sign of Jeremy, but that might be a good thing. What would she say when he walked in and saw her flustered and red-faced? Oh, God, a trickle of sweat was now dripping down the back of her neck. She pulled in a breath and turned back to Sam. "What a small world," she said.

"That it is," he said smoothly, flashing that irresistible smile.

She narrowed her gaze. It was so easy for him. *Too* easy for him.

"Still in advertising?" Boy, that was lame. Sam wasn't just in advertising. Sam *was* advertising.

An amused flicker caught Sam's eyes, but he replied with a simple, "Yep."

"Business going well?" she asked, a little more pertly than she'd wished. For years after he'd so ceremoniously dumped her, she'd fantasized about this exact situation. What she'd be wearing. How her hair would be parted. What she'd say. She'd hoped to have a big rock on her finger by then, given to her by someone who actually cared. She'd laugh away his concerns over how things had ended, flit her wrist when he showed some remorse, and make it damn clear she was over him, when in fact, she still wasn't.

"Very well." Sam gave a lopsided smile and motioned

to her attire. "And yourself?"

Lila felt an old wound begin to tear open. "I'm doing quite well. I'm a freelance copywriter now, actually."

"For agencies or directly with clients?"

"A little of both." She was proud of her work, proud of how far she'd come since that little blip in New York.

"Better than working for a boss?" Sam's smile turned rueful.

Better than working for you, she thought. "I enjoy it. In fact, I have a meeting shortly with Reed Sugar. I'm sure you've heard of them," she added with a faint smile.

Her eyes flitted once more to the door, just in time to see Jeremy Reed walk up to the hostess. In tow was an older man with Jeremy's same features, presumably his father, as well as two other well-suited executives. Her stomach tensed. What now?

She looked at Sam, ready to make her excuse, to say good-bye for good this time. To forget this little run-in had never occurred. To get back to her life and the people that mattered. "Sam, I—"

"Sam Crawford!" Jeremy boomed, bypassing her completely. His stride was long, the smile on his face genuine, and he took Sam's hand in a firm shake. "Jeremy Reed."

Lila blinked rapidly, noticing that Sam didn't seem at all surprised by the introduction. Before she could wrap her head around what was happening, she was shaking hands and making small talk with some other men, all the while smiling as if nothing was amiss.

"All here?" The hostess grinned over Jeremy's shoulder.

Lila fell back behind the Reed team, her mind racing as her feet wove a path through the tables. Stealing her chance before they were seated, she hissed over her shoulder to Sam, "Did you—"

"I had no idea," he whispered back, and something in the urgency of his tone told her he was just as unhappy about the situation as she was.

∗

Jeremy settled back in his chair and glanced from Lila to Sam. "Do you two already know each other?"

Was it that obvious? Lila inwardly groaned, and forced a brighter smile.

"Lila and I used to work together, actually," Sam said tightly as he scanned the menu.

"What a small world," Jeremy chuckled.

A small world, indeed. Lila twisted the heavy cloth napkin in her lap, wishing it was paper, so she could rip it into shreds instead. When she'd started her day she could never have known that a few hours later she would be sitting next to her ex-boyfriend, of all people. Every day she made a conscious effort not to think about him. To look forward. Not back. And here he was. On her turf. In her city. In her big meeting.

The past six years had come undone in the five minutes since he'd walked in that door.

"I imagine you're wondering why I brought you both in for this," Jeremy began.

You could say that again. Lila leaned across the table, noting with a slight frown that Sam was casually sitting back in his chair, a smug smile playing at his lips. This was just another day at the office for him, another client to land amongst his many others. He didn't care as much as she did. He didn't need this as badly as she did. Sam was raised with a silver spoon; he couldn't begin to imagine what it felt like to work for something out of necessity, not greed.

The knot in her stomach tensed when she thought of what was riding on her winning this account. She couldn't let them see how much she needed this. Not with Sam sitting there looking like he could take it or leave it.

"Everyone who is anyone knows the name Crawford and advertising go hand in hand," said Jeremy's father, Mitch Reed, and Lila squeezed the napkin a little harder. This wasn't looking good. "But I'm a traditionalist. I like to keep business here in Chicago where Reed Sugar was founded."

Lila's pulse skipped with interest. She slanted a glance at Sam as she wiggled her back straighter against her chair.

"Lila, we like your portfolio, and Jeremy speaks very highly of you."

Lila slid her old friend a grateful smile.

"Which is why we'd like you to team up on this,"

Mitch finished.

Lila sat in silence. Work with Sam? No way, never again. She'd been down that road and look where it had landed her. Broke and heartbroken. A miserable combination.

"So what do you think?" Jeremy asked expectantly. All eyes from the Reed Sugar team were on them. "I'm sure PC Advertising uses freelancers."

"Occasionally," Sam said diplomatically, "but we prefer to keep things in house. And without any offense to Lila . . ." He flashed her an apologetic shrug before returning his focus to Mitch Reed. "This is the big leagues, gentlemen."

"No offense taken, Sam." Lila gave a cool smile, but narrowed her eyes just enough to make sure he saw the fury glistening in her pupils. She paused, stifling a wince at what she was about to say as she turned back to Mitch. "Having had the . . . *honor* of working with Sam in the past, I must tell you that my creative vision differs slightly from his."

Jeremy cut his hand through the air dismissively. "I'm sure you'll put your heads together and come up with something brilliant."

"PC Advertising has excellent copywriters on staff," Sam stated bluntly.

Lila felt her brow pinch. If he was trying to steal this opportunity from her, then she was prepared to put up a fight. She gave him a long, hard look. She wouldn't put it past him.

"If you're worried about the financial breakdown, we have that covered," Jeremy said. "It's competitive and fair and not something I can imagine either of you turning down."

Sam held up a hand politely, about to protest again, no doubt, when he was cut off by Mitch Reed. "I've been hearing some interesting rumors about your agency recently. Something to do with a certain chain?"

Lila frowned in confusion. Beside her, Sam froze in his chair. Loosening his silk tie, he released a deep, low chuckle.

"You're good," Sam admitted with a knowing smile.

"We know we're good," Jeremy said. "And that's why we want the best. You are still the best, aren't you, Mr. Crawford?"

"What exactly are you proposing?" Sam asked crisply.

"Show us what you can come up with and let's meet again in two weeks," Mitch replied.

A tense pause ensued. Eventually, Sam tossed up his hands and turned to Lila. "What do you say?" he asked, throwing her a casual wink that caused her heart to reflexively lurch. "For old times?"

All eyes bored into her, waiting for her response. She stared at Sam, wide-eyed, searching his gaze for a hint of mockery and startling at the uncertainty she saw briefly shadow his face. Was he seriously agreeing to this ludicrous proposition? Because he needed it or because he'd rather work with her than walk away and let her have it? She couldn't be sure, but the flicker that passed through his gaze only confirmed her suspicion. Something was up, and Sam wasn't going to turn away this chance.

Well, neither was she.

Lila struggled to form the words, wishing there was something, anything she could say to avoid having to work with Sam, but she knew it was hopeless. She wasn't in a position to turn down this opportunity, and another one wasn't likely to just fall into her lap anytime soon.

Mitch tented his hands on the table. "Some might call this an opportunity of a lifetime."

Never had a phrase filled with so much hope felt like such a burden.

An opportunity of a lifetime. That's what it was, all right. And no one, especially Sam Crawford of all people, was going to stop Lila from seizing it.

Chapter Two

Lila waited until she was a safe distance from the restaurant before dropping onto a bench and slowly easing her shoe off her heel. She wiggled her toes and sighed. She knew her sister would be anxiously waiting to hear about the meeting, but she couldn't bring herself to call her just yet. She needed to clear her head first, process what had just happened.

Sam Crawford. It just didn't seem possible!

She hadn't known the last time she saw Sam that it would be her last. Until today. She'd gone to work, the same as any other day, and then . . . *Bam*. No job. No boyfriend. Blindsided.

Well, her eyes were open now. But her heart . . . Her heart was permanently closed to that man. It had to be.

Right. She wedged the shoe back on her aching foot,

gritting her teeth at the pain, and began hobbling down the sidewalk. She'd hoped the walk would clear her head, but it was no use. Her mind was spinning. With images of Sam. With memories of the time they'd spent together. Of the way he looked today.

She took the "L" north, feeling better when she was back in the Lincoln Park neighborhood. With its trendy shops, chic restaurants, and historic brownstones, it was a far cry from the hustle of the Loop, and the primary reason she had chosen to rent office space here. She'd tried the corporate world, but here, she was inspired.

Not yet ready to go back to the office, she stopped for an iced coffee at her favorite café on the corner. It was a daily habit that had turned into a ritual once she became friends with the owner, and no matter how rotten her day was going, she always felt a little brighter after some good coffee and a few laughs.

"The usual?" Hailey asked with a wink as Lila walked up to the counter.

Lila grinned. Usually, she salivated over all the goodies, and then, pouting, opted for a drip coffee with skim milk. Oh, when she had reason to celebrate she selected a pastry, and when she had reason to wallow, she went straight for anything with chocolate, but more often than not, her tip was bigger than her bill.

Lila eyed the display case hungrily, taking in the muffins and cookies she knew Hailey baked fresh each morning. She'd only picked at her lunch, and a chocolate chip scone might help push back the knot that had settled directly in her stomach. "I'll take that scone. And make the coffee a mocha, actually."

"Whipped cream?" Hailey lifted a brow.

"Why not?" Lila sighed. "And the dark chocolate shavings. Extra, if possible."

"Let me guess, one of those days?" Hailey tossed her ponytail over her shoulder as she walked over to the espresso machine.

You could say that again, Lila thought. "On second thought, I'll take one of those brownies, too. For Penny," she added. Her assistant had been looking a bit glum lately. Yet another Internet date gone wrong.

She collected her coffee and the crisp white paper bag and waved good-bye to her friend, wishing she could stay and chat but knowing that she couldn't. It was time to get to work. To focus on figuring out this mess. She wandered slowly back to her office, considerably more deflated than she'd felt just a mere two hours ago when so much had seemed possible.

Now landing the Reed Sugar account felt nothing short of impossible.

"You have a phone call," said Penny as Lila entered the small waiting area that could only hold a writing desk, two visitor chairs, and a sad-looking plant named Fred.

It was probably Mary, asking for details. Lila hated the thought of her sister eying the clock, crossing her fingers, and waiting for the news that could turn her life around. But more than that, she hated the thought of being the one to let her down.

"Just put it through to voice mail, please. I have to go eat my emotions." She reached into the bag and pulled out a fudgy cheesecake brownie. "For you."

"Oh, wow. I needed this," Penny said. "I swear, I'm about ready to just swear off men completely!"

Lila pursed her lips. "Oh, believe me. I understand."

"But the thing is, there is sort of someone new. We've been e-mailing, so . . . you never know!"

Lila tried to give her a smile of encouragement but found it difficult. Her heart felt heavy, her stomach felt sick, and her head was muddled with thoughts of Sam and the pressure to overlook the ache in her chest. She knew that now was the time to focus, to work hard and not back down, but she couldn't stop thinking of those bright blue eyes, that smile, and the way her body seemed to be on high alert, so in tune with his every move.

"I take it the meeting didn't go so well?" Penny asked worriedly.

"Let's just say it didn't go as expected," Lila said.

"Well, this might cheer you up, then," Penny said, waggling her eyebrows. She lowered her voice, as if she and Lila were in on some sort of tantalizing secret together. "The person on the phone is a man by the name of Sam. And he's been holding for nearly *ten* minutes."

Lila forced her expression to remain steady, which wasn't an easy task. How typical of him to omit a last name. As if he was the only Sam in the world.

Sadly, he was the only Sam in *her* world.

"Put it through," she sighed, feeling her shoulders deflate. She watched as Penny pressed a button, set down the receiver, and happily bit into her brownie.

Lila walked into her adjacent office and shut the French doors behind her with a click, wondering just exactly what she would say when she picked up that receiver. Oh, there were several choice words she'd like to say, of course, but then none of them would get her any closer to her goal of winning Reed Sugar's business.

She settled into her chair and let the phone ring twice. The sound seemed to reverberate off the small four walls like an alarm.

"Lila Harris?" she answered in her most crisp and professional tone.

"Lila Harris," Sam said smoothly, and Lila's heart reflexively beat a little faster. Even after everything he had done to her, his voice still had a way of making her body respond all on its own. It was bitterly unfair.

"Oh, hello, Sam," Lila quipped pleasantly, hoping she was successful in keeping her voice from shaking. Under her desk, her stiff, patent leather kitten heels did a nervous tap dance on the floor.

"Cut the formalities, Lila," Sam jumped in. "You knew it was me."

Lila bit back a wave of frustration. He was as cocky as ever, proving to her just how little he had changed. His arrogance was a trait she had found attractive—once. When she was twenty-two and fresh out of college, it was easy to fall for that swag around the office, the confident grin. Now, at twenty-nine, she knew better. "What do you want, Sam?"

"Well, since you're cutting to the chase, I will too. Have dinner with me tonight."

"I can't." The words were out of her mouth before she had time to process them, but nevertheless, they were true. She might not have plans for the evening other than a date with her sister in front of their favorite television show, but that didn't mean she was available for dinner with the guy who had shattered her heart and then stomped all over it.

"Can't or won't?"

Lila sighed in exasperation and looked out her window onto the tree-lined street. Usually she found the view inspiring, sometimes even distracting, but today she barely registered it. "I don't see any point in it."

"No point in it?" Sam parroted. "I'm hurt!"

His lighthearted approach stung; he clearly harbored no remorse, otherwise this wouldn't be so easy for him. God knew it wasn't easy for her.

"Besides," Sam continued, "there is a point in it. If we're going to be working together on this campaign, you're going to have to get used to spending time with me again."

Again. It was a faint acknowledgement of their past. One that he didn't seem to struggle with. Lila knew with a sinking sensation that he was right. She had hoped the majority of their collaboration could be accomplished via e-mail or conference calls, but deep down she had known this was wishful thinking. She closed her eyes and counted to five. "How long are you staying in town?"

"As long as it takes," Sam replied.

Now this was suspicious. "Won't they need you back in New York?"

"Nah. It's a well-oiled machine over there. Besides, if they need me, I can always fly in for the day."

"What about clothes?" She was stalling, she knew, but she didn't care. She had to clear her head, she had to think rationally. She had to stop her heart from pinging every time that smooth, deep voice purred down the line.

"My hotel is right near Michigan Avenue. I can buy a new wardrobe in under an hour. Now, I'll ask you again. Will you have dinner with me tonight?"

It was inevitable, wasn't it? If she didn't have dinner with him tonight, then she'd probably have to see him tomorrow. Better to get it over with, she decided. "Fine," she sighed.

"I knew I'd wear you down." Sam's smirk could be heard through his words, and Lila gripped the phone in agitation.

"I have a knitting class after work," she lied, drawing on the one extra-curricular activity she allowed herself at the cute little yarn shop next door to her office.

"A *knitting* class?" Sam guffawed. Lila listened in seething silence as he chuckled merrily and then said, "I thought only my grandmother did that."

For a split second, Lila was thrown. In all their time together, Sam rarely mentioned his family. Aside from his brother and father, Lila knew nothing of the people in Sam's world. Yet another red flag she'd been hell-bent on overlooking. *Stupid girl.*

Well, she was smarter than that now.

"I can meet you at eight," she said. That would give her enough time to catch up with Mary and manage her sister's expectations. Guiltily, she glanced down at the flashing blue light on the corner of her cell phone. She was doing this for her family, she reminded herself firmly, and somehow that made spending time with Sam tolerable. Almost.

"Eight o'clock it is then," Sam said. "I've heard good things about a place called Harbor House. Sound good to you?"

"Fine," she muttered and placed the receiver back on the cradle without another word. She sat back in her chair, staring at the phone, contemplating the events of the day. In a matter of hours she would be sitting down to dinner with the man who had betrayed her in the worst way possible. She should be disgusted. She should be furious. She should be dreading the very thought of it.

So why was it that she couldn't stop herself from smiling?

*

Sam swiped his key card through the slot, waited for the beep and the click of the lock, and then entered his hotel suite. Loosening his tie, he slipped it over his head and tossed it on a nearby chair, followed by his suit jacket. He'd walked back from lunch, stopping to buy a few things for his extended stay, and he felt sweaty and anxious.

It was going to be a difficult two weeks, and only a few things could take the edge off right now. At this hour in the afternoon, Sam decided his best bet was a long run.

There was a gym in the hotel, but fresh air would clear his head, and from his window he could see the path along the lakefront was already filled with joggers. There were boats in the distance, their sails blowing in the window, some so far out they looked like small red or blue dots bobbing on the water.

He changed quickly, eager to get outside and enjoy a rare break from his routine, when his phone began to vibrate. Cursing under his breath, he reluctantly tapped on the message. His brother had two words for him: *Call me.* It was the seventh text of this nature in the last hour, Sam noted with a frown. Even from eight hundred miles away, he couldn't escape the office.

"What's going on?" he asked when his brother answered his call on the first ring.

"We lost them," Rex said flatly.

Sam sat down on the bed. So it had really happened. Jolt Coffee had been threatening to break their contract for over a month—citing creative differences, even though it was evident they were really looking to cut costs—but Sam never thought they'd end their contract so quickly. Their biggest client. Gone. Just like that. Warning or no warning, it was still a punch in the gut.

"Who are they going with?"

"It hasn't been announced yet." Rex's voice was thick with tension. The implications of losing Jolt Coffee were endless. The media would have a field day with this; the chosen firm would garner immediate attention and respect. At their expense.

"So we have some time then," Sam mused aloud.

"Every account manager is feeling out the status of their clients right now. But when this hits . . ."

"There are going to be questions," Sam finished. No doubt, other clients would wonder why things fell apart.

Rex groaned. "How did the meeting with Reed go?"

"They're definitely eager to use us," Sam said, omitting to mention that Reed had already heard rumors of Jolt Coffee taking their business elsewhere. "But they have a slightly unconventional way of wanting to go about it."

"What do you mean?"

"They want us to use a freelance copywriter." Sam paused. "Do you happen to recall Lila Harris?"

Sam wasn't surprised to hear Rex reply, "No."

"She was a copywriter for us about six and a half years ago."

There was a pause. "Brown hair, long legs, nice smile?"

Sam swallowed. If he let himself, he could still remember the warmth between her thighs when he—

"Yes, that's her."

"I remember her. You took a liking to her. Pretty girl," Rex said. More sharply he added, "I also remember she had no vision, she was headstrong, and Dad fired her. And now you're telling me that Reed Sugar wants us to use her as our copywriter?"

"So they said," Sam said, his stomach tightening.

"Dad will never go for this."

Sam crossed to the window and stared out at the view. Preston Crawford may have technically retired from the day to day work at the firm, but the agency was still his legacy, his namesake. More than Sam himself had ever been, Sam thought darkly.

He turned away from the window. "And if it's this or nothing?"

After another heavy pause, Rex asked, "What did they propose?"

"They want to see something in two weeks."

"Two weeks." The words hung in the air. Both men knew how much could happen in such a relatively short amount of time. Jolt Coffee could make an announcement tomorrow, for all they knew, and in this industry, your reputation was built on the caliber of your clients.

"Need me back before then?" Sam asked as an image of Lila immediately formed. He tossed it aside just as quickly. He couldn't afford a distraction now.

"We need you where you are," Rex replied. "Reed Sugar could be the deciding factor in whether this agency sinks or swims. Do whatever it takes to make sure we get that account."

Sam ended the call and canceled his return flight, happy to avoid going back to New York tomorrow. The office was tense, the pressure high, and the stakes . . . even higher. He knew what people thought of him— overly ambitious, cutthroat, heartless even—but they didn't know why. If they did . . . Well, if they did they'd look at him a little differently, and he'd be out of the game.

For the thousandth time he reminded himself of this. No one, not even Lila, could know the details of his past. It had been difficult to keep so much from her when they were dating. All he'd wanted to do was get close, open up, but the little voice in his head held him back, reminding him of all he stood to lose. He'd fought too hard to get where he was just to end up at square one.

That's what he told himself, at least.

Sam tossed the phone on the bed and grabbed his room key. He needed to run, far and fast, and shake these racing thoughts from his head. He should be thinking about Reed right now, and everyone who was depending on him back in New York. But all he could think about was Lila. The way she used to sigh his name first thing in the morning, pressing her warm skin close against his chest, her hair tickling his face. The sound of her laugh when he'd chase her through the rain, all the way back to that tiny little studio apartment she was renting in Brooklyn.

The way she looked at him one last time, all those years ago, her eyes dark with hurt. And the way he felt, standing in that cold boardroom, watching her go, and knowing, with sinking admission, that no matter how badly he wanted to, he couldn't go after her.

*

Mary was standing in the vestibule of their apartment building, flipping through her mail and tossing flyers into the bin, when Lila came home that evening.

"Hey there," she said with a smile that lit up her entire face. "How was the meeting?"

Lila hated the hope she saw in her younger sister's expression. Mary had given up a lot over the years, never giving the impression that she was making a sacrifice, and in all that time she'd never vocalized a wish for more than she had. Until recently.

When Gramps died four months ago, they inherited their grandparents' wedding china, a collection of photo albums and vintage furniture, the cuckoo clock, an alarming amount of debt, and, of course, Sunshine Creamery, the family's ice cream parlor. As much as Lila hated the thought of selling the place, it was old and tired and in dire need of a renovation neither of them could afford.

She'd expected her sister to reach the same conclusion, but instead Mary had begged Lila to find a way. Any way. Lila understood. Sunshine Creamery, with its Formica counters, mint green walls, and faded pink-striped awning, was the last connection they had to their past, to any family outside each other. They'd grown up in that place, dishing out sundaes during summer break, sneaking maraschino cherries from the bowl in the fridge, watching their grandparents, and later, just their grandfather mix the creamy concoctions and store them in carefully labeled cardboard containers in the freezer.

And because it was Mary who had dropped out of college to take care of their grandmother when she was sick, and later sat by her grandfather's hospital bed and promised she would keep the family tradition alive, and because it was Mary who had curled up with her in bed all those cold winter nights when they were children, begging to be told stories of the parents she couldn't even remember, because Lila had gotten two extra years with them, after all; Lila had decided then and there that she would find a way to keep the ice cream parlor.

Everything was riding on landing this big account. If she didn't pull through, she wasn't sure how she'd ever live with herself.

"It was . . . okay," Lila said with a reluctant smile. She glanced at the mail with the same eagerness she always had as a child, when the thought of a letter seemed so thrilling. Now, most of the mail she received came in the form of a bill, especially since their grandfather had died. "They want to meet again in two weeks."

"See, I knew it!" Mary's grin broadened.

"It's not a done deal yet," Lila warned as she began

climbing the stairs.

"But it sounds like it could be! I've been thinking, and I bet I could do a lot of the renovation myself. Then I wouldn't have to borrow so much." Mary currently worked thirty hours a week as a receptionist at a doctor's office, and she'd just taken another part-time job to pick up some extra hours. Lila had offered her some work in her office, but Mary insisted it was better this way. She'd flitted through jobs, never sticking with one—never showing much passion until Sunshine Creamery became a possibility.

Lila's heart tugged. Her sister deserved to have something of her own, just like she did, and what better than the ice cream parlor? With any luck, one of them would have a child to pass it down to one day. That is, if either of them could ever find a guy worth settling down with. So far, the best Lila had fared was Sam, and Mary, well, she was still skirting her boss's advances.

Lila paused at the landing and gave her sister a hard look. "You're not *borrowing* anything. It's a family business. You're my family." *My only family,* she finished silently.

Mary gave her a quick hug. "So tell me everything. We'll splurge and order a pizza."

Lila's smile felt wan. As much as she would have loved to toss on her favorite pajamas and relax at the little bistro table she and Mary had set up on the fire escape, she had to get ready to meet Sam, and she didn't have a clue what she should wear.

"I have a dinner thing tonight," she said.

Mary studied her with interest. "Oh, do you now?"

"It's not like that," Lila replied, but her voice lacked conviction. Who was she kidding? She didn't know what this dinner would be like, what to prepare herself for. *The worst*, she decided. It was her only protection. "It's a business thing."

Mary's eyes narrowed as she nodded her head. "A thing," she repeated softly.

Lila laughed. "Come on. I'll tell you everything while I get ready." *Well, almost everything*, she thought. Plucking her key from her pocket, she unlocked the door, feeling her shoulders relax as it swung open. Home. After six years, this really was her home—with no other to return to by now. Modest at best, and some might say downright cramped, to Lila it was perfect. Especially on a day like today.

Dropping her tote in the small entranceway, she kicked off the flip-flops she'd changed into after that disastrous meeting and wandered into the living room, Mary footsteps behind. Of the four rooms in the apartment, this was her favorite, with its exposed brick wall and antique fireplace that was more for display than use. Lila loved nothing more than to curl up with a good book in the slip-covered chair near the tall bay window.

But there wouldn't be any of that tonight. Tonight she had a date. A meeting! Yes, a *meeting*.

"I should probably get in the shower," she said, but

her feet stayed planted to the floor.

"I'll make some iced tea," Mary offered. With a sly grin, she ducked into the kitchen.

Lila went into the bathroom and turned on the taps, feeling immediately better when the hot water hit her skin. Nothing like a shower and a chat with her sister to calm her down. And with less than an hour before she'd be sitting across a table from the one man who had the power to stir her emotions like none other, she needed all the help she could get.

Mary was standing in the kitchen, leaning against the doorjamb to the hall, when Lila emerged in her terrycloth robe a few minutes later. "Details. Now."

Lila accepted the glass of iced tea and followed her sister onto their makeshift balcony. Instead of sitting down, she went over to the flower box they'd hung over the rail and inspected their herb garden. Behind her, Mary made a show of clearing her throat.

She supposed she couldn't put it off forever. Mary had a way of seeing right through her, and there was no way Lila would be able to hide her feelings today. "Do you remember that guy I told you about from my days in New York? Sam?"

Mary's eyes were so wide, Lila could see the white around her brown irises. "Yes . . ." She blinked rapidly.

"Well, he's sort of the person I'm meeting tonight," Lila muttered.

"Are you kidding me?" Mary squealed. She swept her

long auburn hair from her face and wrapped a band from her wrist around and around until she had formed a careless knot on top of her head. "You're having dinner with Sam tonight. *The* Sam. Where's he taking you?"

Lila hesitated. "Harbor House."

"The most romantic restaurant in town," Mary pointed out.

Lila pinched her lips and set the glass of tea on the table. Sam had stumbled back into her life after all these years, not by choice, but by chance. He hadn't sought her out. He hadn't tried to right his wrongs. And he certainly didn't have any emotional interest in her. Clearly, he never had.

Why couldn't they meet somewhere else? Like a conference room?

"I'm sorry," Mary interrupted her thoughts. "Am I missing something here? This is Sam, right? The same Sam you pined for—"

"You're forgetting what he did to me." Lila turned back to the bed of herbs. They looked just as wilted as she felt.

Mary grew silent as Lila took the watering can into the kitchen. Anger stirred within her as she waited for it to fill with water. Sam was a jerk. A horrible, selfish person. *Just remember that*, she told herself. She'd chant it all through dinner.

She glanced at her sister through the screen door before returning to the balcony. Mary always grounded her, ever since they were little. It was why she chose to share this apartment after coming back to Chicago. Sure, she could have afforded a place of her own, but how lonely would that be? She'd needed to get back to her roots after the disappointment of New York. She needed to focus on what was important. And *who* was important.

Lila gave the herbs a long bath and returned the watering can to its corner. She glanced at her watch. Her pulse kicked up a notch when she saw the time. "I should probably get ready."

Mary followed her through the sunny white kitchen and into the bedroom Lila had painted a soothing shade of blue. She'd read somewhere it was a tranquil color, meant to calm. Today, however, it wasn't living up to its reputation.

"I still don't understand how this all happened. I thought today was your big meeting with Reed Sugar."

"It was." Lila riffled through her closet, finally deciding on a gray pencil skirt and a black, short-sleeved blouse. If she told her sister that winning the account hinged on collaborating with Sam, there was no doubt that alarm would quickly follow. She wasn't ready to let Mary down until she had to, and with any luck, it wouldn't come to that. "I ran into Sam while I was waiting for the meeting to start. He's in town for business and . . . well, we're bouncing some ideas off each other."

Mary's lip curled as Lila tossed the clothes onto the bed. "Please tell me you're not planning to wear that."

"I told you," Lila insisted, "that this is not a date!"

"I don't understand why you keep saying that!" Mary shook her head. "You were crazy about this man! And now here he is . . . all these years later. You thought you would never see him again!"

"Exactly." Lila gritted her teeth. She had gone out of her way never to see him again. How could life be so cruel?

"You're honestly telling me that there isn't a part of you that's glad to see him?" Mary pressed. "A tiny part of you?"

Lila stared at her sister, stricken. "No, Mary. No!" she repeated with emphasis. She was shaking as she stuffed the skirt back into her closet and pulled out a scoop neck dress that hit safely below the knee.

Mary reached for the next hanger and held up a black, spaghetti strap shift dress with a slit up the back.

"No," Lila said.

"*Yes*," Mary insisted. "Why shouldn't he see you at your best? This is your chance, Lila!"

Mary was right about that. It *was* her chance. And she wasn't going to mess it up by getting any romantic notions.

Still, she thought, eyeing the dress, in her revenge fantasy, she *had* been looking fabulous, with fresh highlights, perfectly toned abs and calves, and skin that hadn't aged a day. The least she could do was wear the damn dress.

"Maybe he's sorry," Mary suggested as Lila fumbled with the zipper.

"No, if he was sorry he could have apologized to me a long time ago."

Mary's smile was one of encouragement. "Maybe he's changed."

Lila tipped her chin. Oh, Mary. The eternal optimist. "People don't change," she said firmly. And she'd be wise to remember that, no matter what he had up his sleeve for tonight.

Lila stared in the mirror and felt her shoulders droop. Her hair was still damp, hanging at her sun-kissed shoulders, which were on full display along with her arms and legs and half her chest. There was entirely too much skin being shown, even if it was almost July, and even if she was twenty-nine. And even if she was having dinner with the hottest guy she'd ever kissed.

Make that the *meanest* guy she'd ever kissed.

"I look like I care," she sighed.

"You do and you should," Mary said, coming up behind her. "Show him what he's been missing. Remind him of the biggest mistake of his life."

Lila grinned. Mary had a point. Still, she swiped her eyeglasses from her dresser and slid them on. Just in case there was any misunderstanding that this meeting was anything but professional.

Chapter Three

Lila stared warily at the stone façade of Harbor House from across the street. It was hardly the type of place you went to with a business colleague. With its small, candlelit tables and view of the water, Harbor House was exactly the kind of place you went to get engaged, not suffer through a dinner with an old flame you desperately wanted to forget.

The sun was on its last breath, tucking behind the horizon, leaving an orange cast to the sky in its wake. A cool breeze was blowing off the lake, and Lila tucked her hair behind her ears as she crossed the street, taking time with each step. She should have told him they could meet tomorrow, at her office, where Penny could chaperone. That's what she should have done. But all it had taken was thirty seconds of Sam's charm and she was fuzzy headed, barely able to think ahead to the consequences of her own knee-jerk reactions to his whims.

Well, not tonight, she told herself firmly, as she approached the quaint little restaurant tucked alongside one of the city's harbors. Tonight there would be no forgetting the past. And no discussing it either. The last thing she needed was to be derailed from the business at hand.

Inside the restaurant, the dining room was airy, with square tables covered in crisp white tablecloths. The hostess motioned to the outdoor patio, and there he was, sitting on a wrought iron chair, looking out over the water, one foot hooked on the other knee, arms casually bent on chair rests, his sunglasses folded neatly on the table. Not a care in the world.

So this was how it was going to be. Now, after all this time. As if nothing had ever gone on between the two of them.

Lila lifted her chin and walked onto the sweeping deck, taking in the strings of lights that hung from the whitewashed portico, and the colorful flowers nestled in whiskey barrels, trying in vain to focus on anything but the man in the pink polo and navy shorts with the electric blue eyes who knew how to kiss her until she moaned.

"Hello again," she said as she took her seat across from him.

God, he looked good tonight. Too good.

He's a jerk, Lila. A horrible, selfish person.

Having risen to meet her, Sam sat back down in his chair and smiled until his eyes crinkled at the corners. Lila quickly averted her gaze to the menu. He didn't need to look so happy. As if nothing had ever transpired.

"You look nice," Sam said through a warm smile, and Lila gritted her teeth. He was smooth. Too smooth. So smooth that it was easy to just believe anything he said and fall under his spell.

He's a jerk, Lila. A horrible, selfish person.

She skimmed the menu, not registering any of the words. She rarely wore her glasses—they were a weak prescription used for reading—and the glare of the sunset was blinding, causing her to blink.

But to take them off now . . .

"I'm glad you agreed to meet me tonight," Sam continued. "I wasn't sure you would."

Lila set down the menu and twisted the napkin in her lap, torn between relaxing into the night with the one man whose conversation she had enjoyed above all others at one time, and keeping up the protective wall she had built for herself since moving back to Chicago. She searched his handsome face for a glimmer of menace, a concrete reminder of what he had done to her, and came up blank. All she saw across from her was the man who had captured her heart.

And then broke it.

"I took the liberty of ordering us a bottle of wine," Sam said, his voice low and rich. "I remembered you like Cabernet."

"I do," Lila said, raising her eyes to boldly meet his, "but I prefer white in the summer." But then, how would he have known that? They'd never made it to the summer. Their relationship—if that's what it ever was—had started in September and ended in March. Six sweet months.

Sam chuckled and reached for his water glass. It was wet with condensation. "You're not going to make this easy for me, are you?"

She tipped her head. "And why should I?"

"I'm going to give you a good time tonight," Sam said, shaking a playful finger at her across the table. "Whether you like it or not."

Go ahead and try. But despite her resolve, she couldn't resist the thrill of excitement that bubbled inside her. There was still something there. A spark. Maybe just an attraction. Or maybe it was history. There was no escaping that.

She stalled to compose herself before daring to reply, grateful for the interruption of the server uncorking a wine bottle with a decorative French label. If Sam was here to apologize, he had a poor way of handling it. Their past was too big to be swept under the rug. Some things couldn't be forgiven. Or forgotten.

"A toast," Sam announced, raising his glass.

Lila hesitated, sighed, and then reluctantly held up her own glass. The evening was already getting off track. She was going against her own intentions and getting emotional. This was business. Nothing more.

"To old friends," Sam said. He took a slow sip, winking at her over the rim of his glass.

Lila's blood boiled as she glared at the sparkle in his eye. Wordlessly, she took a sip of the smooth wine. Across from her, Sam watched to see if she enjoyed his selection. She'd be damned if she gave him the satisfaction.

She set the wine on the table and pushed her glasses up her nose with her index finger. "I suppose we should discuss Reed Sugar, seeing as we only have two weeks to come up with something spectacular."

Sam opened the menu and studied it for a few seconds before asking, "Do you have any initial ideas?"

"A few," she lied, having been too distracted all day to form a coherent thought. "It might be best to go over some visuals in my office tomorrow. Would two o'clock work for you?"

Sam pulled his phone from his pocket and tapped a few buttons. "Ten would be better."

Lila didn't bother to check her calendar before replying steadily, "How does two thirty work?"

Sam's eyes locked hers, gauging her intention. "That will be just fine," he said evenly.

"I look forward to it then," Lila said, flashing her first smile of the evening.

"As do I." Sam closed his menu firmly. He hunched forward across the table, closing the distance between them. "But enough talk about business, Lila. You and I both know why we're here."

Lila's heart began to race. "I don't know about you, but I'm here to discuss sugar."

Sam regarded her levelly. "You're still upset about our misunderstanding. Lila, that was more than half a decade ago!"

"Misunderstanding?" Lila felt her jaw slack. "There was no *misunderstanding*, Sam. I lost my job—"

"And how was that my fault, exactly?" Sam countered.

"Amazing." Lila shook her head in disgust. "You really take no responsibility for it at all, do you?"

Sam squinted at the accusation. "I wasn't the one who fired you."

"No, you weren't," she agreed, frowning as she thought of Sam's father. "But you didn't do anything to try to stop it, either."

"That's not fair," Sam said.

Disbelief quickly turned to anger, and Lila felt a slow heat creep up her cheeks. "Your father fired me, Sam. And you let him do it!"

His jaw pulsed. "Explain to me what I could have done differently."

"You set me up to fail, Sam. You brought me in on that toothpaste campaign, and then you shot down every idea I had."

"Lila . . ." Sam sighed wearily. He closed his eyes and pinched the bridge of his nose with his thumb and forefinger, grimacing.

"But then, to sweeten the deal, you never bothered to call. We'd been dating for six months, Sam. Was I just left to assume it was over? Job and boyfriend? One fell swoop? Did you just decide one day you'd grown bored with me? Let your daddy do your dirty work?" She'd said far more than she'd ever wanted to say, but now that it was out, she felt a strange sense of relief. He'd hurt her. Why hide it?

With a shaking hand, Lila reached for her wine glass and took a long sip. And then another. She needed to calm down; things had gone too far in too short an amount of time.

The waitress arrived at their table, ready to take their orders. Already forgetting what she'd decided on, Lila flipped open the menu and, struggling to see through the glare of her glasses, took them off in frustration and settled on the risotto. Sam watched all this with a twitch in his lips, waiting until the server had left before saying. "I was sort of liking the sexy librarian look."

Lila felt her back teeth graze. Enough was enough. Nothing he could say could lighten the mood. Nothing he could say could undo what he'd done.

Lila placed her napkin on the table. "I'm sorry, Sam, but I think I should leave. This . . . this wasn't a good idea." In fact, it was a terrible idea. Just as terrible as the one where she thought she could actually work with this impossible man again. How had her life come so full circle? Once again, her fate was in Sam's hands. Of all people.

"Wait." Sam placed a firm hand on her wrist, forcing her to stop. It had been so long since he'd touched her, but his skin felt familiar—soft and warm. Right.

Wrong. She snatched herself from his grip, and set her hands on her hips. People at nearby tables were no doubt staring by now, but she didn't care. All she cared about was the way Sam looked tonight, and the way that made her feel. She wanted to hate him, but a bigger part of her just *wanted* him. Why couldn't she have found a nice attractive man by now? *Nice* being the operative word.

"I'm sorry I upset you. It wasn't my intention. Really."

Sam's lips were spread thin with displeasure, but his eyes were soft. Lila hesitated ever so briefly before feeling her own features relax and her shoulders loosen.

"We used to have fun once, Lila. Didn't we?"

Lila gave a sad smile and lowered her eyes, thinking back fondly on the laughter they had once shared, the way her breath caught every time he put his hand on the small of her back, the way her heart skipped a beat when he entered a room. "We did," she admitted, and then stopped herself right there.

"Did you know I have a boat?" Sam mused, looking out over the harbor. Before she could reply that no, she did not, because Sam had never really shared much about his life but somehow she had overlooked this major red flag, he said, "I keep it on the Cape. At our beach house. I always wanted to take you on it sometime."

Why was he telling her this? She frowned and waited

until she had found the right words before replying. "You stopped seeing me, Sam. You didn't call, you didn't come over. You didn't even end things. You were just . . . gone."

"It was complicated, Lila." He sighed, and his eyes turned a little flat.

"But you can't say those types of things now. You can't talk about things we might have done. You made a choice."

He opened his mouth as if he was about to argue with her and then, after a pause, closed it again. "You're right. I made a choice." He shrugged. "Some things just aren't meant to be, I guess."

Lila folded her arms across her chest, feeling a heavy weight of disappointment settle in. "No. They're not."

"Will you at least sit down?" Sam pointed to the chair. Lila didn't flinch. "Look, you're stuck with me for at least another two weeks," Sam continued. "After that you never have to see me again. If we land the account, I'll make sure we divide up the work so you do your share and I do mine. And Lila," he added pointedly, forcing her eyes to his. "I intend to win this account."

At this, Lila sat back down. "I intend to win the account, too." She was proud of the work she did, the loyal clients, the steady income, but this was different. This was an opportunity of a lifetime, as Mitch Reed had been so quick to point out.

"So what do you say we make the best of our time together?" Sam raised an eyebrow. Perhaps it was an invitation, perhaps it was a challenge. Either way, it was clear that he wasn't going to take no for an answer.

The thought of never seeing Sam again left a knot in the pit of her stomach. She hadn't allowed herself to miss him for a long time; hating him had been so much easier.

Thousands of men were handsome, she reminded herself. Movie stars were a prime example. It didn't mean you had to go weak in the knees when they behaved badly.

"Two weeks. How hard can it be?" she asked, and managed to force back that little flutter that threatened to release when he flashed her a grin.

Sam may have made millions off his powers of persuasion, but it would take more than a dazzling smile to win her over again.

Chapter Four

Sam wiped the sweat from his brow with the back of his hand. Panting for breath, he set a foot on a wooden park bench and tightened the laces on his running shoes. It was a cool morning, damp from a midnight rain, and few people were out at this time of day. He was still running on East Coast time, up too early, left to pace his hotel room. He'd been out the door at the first sign of daybreak and clocked his seven miles at a personal best, his feet doing overtime to keep up with his racing thoughts.

He'd been up since three, meaning he'd managed four hours of sleep after returning from dinner with Lila—it had taken a good hour to relax enough to drift off.

The recollection of her in that little black number last night still made him squirm with pleasure even now. The girl he knew back in New York didn't dress that way, but then, that girl had turned into a woman, hadn't she? But even though she appeared so different at first glance, she was still the same Lila underneath. He'd seen it shine through once she allowed herself to enjoy dinner last night. The laughter. The quick wit. The warmth in those eyes. That stubborn streak. The way she could disarm him with a curl of her smile. It was all still there.

He could still remember the first time he'd seen her. She strolled into his office all fresh faced and eager, looking for a file. She'd introduced herself and held out a hand, not knowing at the time who he was or what his last name was. That he was a Crawford. He'd kept it that way when he asked her how her first day was going and invited her to sit. Perhaps because she was young, perhaps because she needed a friend, or perhaps because his smile was so genuine, she'd sat down and gratefully poured her heart out to him. He listened as she told him about how nervous she was, how she couldn't believe how small apartments were in the city, how she didn't even know the code to the bathroom. She reminded him of the way he had felt on his first day on the job three years earlier—out of place. A sentiment no one on staff could ever assume coming from the boss's son.

She was sweet, special, and incredibly sexy. She was the one woman who had succeeded in getting under his skin and lingering there. All these years. Just out of reach.

But it didn't matter how he felt. Lila clearly had an

opinion of him, and it wasn't a good one.

Sam's gut tightened as he remembered the impossible position she had left him in all those years before. His father was notorious for hiring and firing new graduates; they had a few months to impress him, and if they didn't succeed, they were out. There was no learning curve. No second chance. Not even for Sam. *Especially* for Sam. The son with the uphill climb. The son who had to prove himself. The son who had to earn his birthright.

He reached the southern edge of Lincoln Park and began walking down Lake Shore Drive. At six thirty in the morning, the luxury apartment buildings to his right were still dark; the doormen visible through the lobby windows looked tired and bored. Up ahead, skyscrapers loomed high above him, the sidewalk turning wide and vacant as he neared Michigan Avenue. Few places would be open for breakfast this hour, and with a curl of his lip, Sam noticed a Jolt Coffee storefront across the street.

Three years had gone into that account. Endless commercials, meetings, catchy new taglines. He used to feel like a traitor for not exclusively drinking their coffee. Now he felt like a traitor for even considering it.

Deciding to go back to the hotel and order room service, Sam jogged the rest of the way. It was almost eight by now in New York, and anything could be unfolding at the office. As soon as he was in his room, he turned on the morning news, listening to the headlines while he skimmed the Internet. Nothing about Jolt Coffee popped up. Hopefully this meant they had bought themselves another day. They'd need thirteen more of those to really be in the clear, though. Ideally, they'd announce the Reed Sugar account before talk of Jolt Coffee hit the industry rags.

Satisfied, he called his brother. "Rex, it's Sam." He wedged his phone between his chin and shoulder and pulled off his running shoes. "Anything new?"

"No buzz here." Rex's voice was scratchy, an indication he hadn't slept.

"Do we have a press release ready yet?"

"Just looking over the draft now. They want a direct quote from you on talks with Reed Sugar. Tell them how sweet it is, Sam."

Sam chewed at his bottom lip. "I hate to drop their name before the deal has been signed. If something goes wrong at the last minute and we don't get the account, we'll end up looking worse."

The phone was silent on the other end. Confused, Sam pulled the device from the crook of his neck and studied the screen. He was still connected. "Rex?"

"Nothing can go wrong, Sam," Rex said bluntly, his tone deceptively calm.

A familiar knot formed in Sam's stomach and settled itself like a heavy weight. It had taken a long time for Rex to warm up to him and even longer to accept Sam as a player in the family business. Sam had worked hard for his brother's support, and somewhere along the line Rex had backed down, looked over the wall he had built up. It was expected that there would be animosity—Rex considered himself the legitimate son, thought of Sam as the black sheep. To Rex, Sam had come out of nowhere, claiming what was his. *Fighting for it.*

Sibling rivalry was not lost on the two brothers, especially when it came to the agency. Rex still struggled with the transition of joint partnership; if it had been up to Rex, he probably would have overseen the agency on his own, with Sam as second in command. Or possibly, not in the picture at all.

Sam stayed firm. "I won't go on record naming Reed until we've signed them. If you need a quote, have them say something like we're in final discussions with a major household brand . . . you follow?"

"I'll be in touch," Rex said wearily.

Sam set the phone on the desk and peeled his sweaty shirt from his back. If he'd learned anything since yesterday, it was that Lila was determined to prove something to him. If she was willing to go so far as to put her pride before the success of this campaign, she'd leave him no other choice, just like she had six years ago.

He had fought too hard for too many years to prove himself as a Crawford. It had taken him twenty years to find his family—and nothing, not even Lila, could stand in his way of belonging to them.

*

She was thinking about Sam again. Not about the way he'd stood coldly in his sleek New York office building and watched her walk out of his life, but about the way he'd looked last night with his lazy smile and kind eyes. Like the guy she'd fallen in love with, not the guy who'd let her down.

She could still feel the heat of his gaze on her when he'd put her into the cab, and then watched as she gave the driver her address, his hands thrust deep in his pockets, his jaw set. She shouldn't be thinking of him like this, she knew. She shouldn't be thinking of him at all! She should be thinking of her sister, and that empty storefront that never should have gone dark.

She glanced at the clock in the bottom left corner of her computer screen. She had less than half an hour to pull herself together and shed all thoughts of Sam's rugged good looks from her mind. There was simply no time for girlish crushes. She was a professional businesswoman with a make it or break it account at stake. If she blew her career over thoughts of Sam, she'd have no one to blame but herself. *Fool me once, shame on you. Fool me twice* . . . There would be no fooling her this time.

Lila opened her files and began organizing herself for the meeting. Sugar. Sweet. Used in pretty much everything. Pure. Raw. Cake. Cookies.

She smiled. *Ice cream.*

She furiously scribbled some ideas in her notebook, her hand barely able to keep up with her mind, until a knock at the door interrupted her.

"He's gorgeous!" Penny hissed.

'Who is?" Lila inquired, though she sensed she already knew the answer.

"Sam Crawford!" Penny whispered gleefully, closing the door carefully behind her. Lila could see the sheen in Penny's bright green eyes. A certain glow that only came about when something unexpected and wonderful collided all at once. A rare gem, so to speak. And Sam was certainly that in the looks department, at least. And in the charm department, as well.

The cad.

Penny had obviously wasted no time in appreciating Sam's natural flirtatious air and good looks. To her credit, she had no idea that Lila ever had anything but a professional connection to him, and Lila decided it best to keep it this way. Drudging up the past would only open old wounds. Besides, none of it mattered anymore. Lila would work with Sam on the Reed Sugar campaign, and in two weeks, he would go back to New York. Just as he said. She'd go back to her life as if this little interruption had never happened, and eventually . . . eventually she would forget about him again. Hopefully.

"Sam." Lila smiled politely as she opened the French doors to the waiting room. Her gaze fell to Fred, who was drooping a little more than usual—an indication that Penny had yet again forgotten to water him.

"Hello," Sam smiled effortlessly, and Lila's pulse skittered.

Get a grip, she scolded herself. Furrowing her brow, she

waved him into her office. It was time to concentrate.

Hot on her heels, Penny flitted nervously with an eager smile said, "Can I get you anything, Sam? Coffee? Water? Tea?" She brought a hand up to her chin-length hair and smoothed it down.

Sam met Lila's eye, fighting off a smile. "I'm fine, thanks."

"Okay." Penny hovered, reluctant to let go of Sam's presence just yet. She turned at the door once more. "Just let me know if you change your mind. I sit right out there. Front desk. Next to the plant."

"Thanks," Sam smiled.

"Thank you, Penny," Lila said, signaling for Penny to close the door behind her. She glanced in Sam's direction, studying him as she spread her notebook on the desk and arranged herself in her chair.

Sam dropped into the visitor's chair. "That plant in your waiting room looks a little sad."

"Please don't insult the man in my life," Lila said briskly, but she struggled to fight off a grin.

"Ah, so there isn't a lucky guy in your world? I'd have thought a girl like you would be snatched up by now."

Lila's eyes narrowed reflexively. He was certainly pleased with himself, wasn't he? No doubt there was a girlfriend in his life. Not that she cared. Not that she cared one bit.

She cleared her throat and glared at Sam. "Ready to begin?"

"Just you and me then?" Sam's eyes twinkled with interest.

Despite her better judgment, Lila's heart flipped at the undertone. "Yep," she replied crisply.

"This is a nice little setup," Sam remarked, sweeping his eyes over the sage green walls and French doors leading back to Penny. And Fred. Lila had selected green as her main color because it was supposed to induce creative thoughts, but she didn't bother telling Sam this. It would only prolong his stay, and the sooner they got this over with, the better. "I thought maybe you worked from home."

"I'm not a hobbyist, Sam. I have a steady client base, and, despite your opinion, I'm good at what I do." Lila waited a beat. "Now, would you like to present your thoughts, or should I go first?" She glanced in his direction, forcing herself to hold his gaze, even if those blue eyes did make her insides go a little mushy. It had been nice, talking to him last night, not about work, not about the past, but just about safe topics . . . food, travel, movies. She'd missed that.

"Ladies first," Sam leaned back in his seat, his hands folded loosely in his lap, as a strange little smile tugged at his mouth.

Lila felt her lips thin in annoyance. Here they were, equals in the eyes of Reed Sugar, and Sam still thought he was the one in charge. Well, he was sorely mistaken.

She shifted in her chair and pressed her shoulders back, reminding herself to stay focused and to not feed in to those sparkling blue eyes or that killer smile that no doubt won him dozens of accounts.

Sam might be the go-to guy in advertising, but he was more trouble than he was worth.

*

Sam watched with growing curiosity as Lila's determination unfolded before him. She had never been good at hiding her emotions, and Sam knew her far too well to be fooled. The lift of her chin, the purse of her lips, and the flash of fury in those hazel eyes were dead giveaways. She was gearing up for a battle, and she wasn't going down without a fight.

"Here, before you begin." Sam stood and walked around the desk, pulling his chair close next to Lila's, watching as her eyes grew wide in alarm. If she wasn't making life so damn difficult at the moment, he'd find her haughty attitude completely irresistible.

"What are you doing?" she asked, her voice a notch higher than usual.

Sam shrugged. He looked around the small room before meeting Lila's blazing stare once more. "This makes it a little easier to put our heads together, so to speak."

With a pinch of her lips, Lila gripped the desk, using it for leverage to help wheel her chair a few inches to her left. God, she was impossible.

And completely irresistible.

"Mitch Reed is a self-confirmed traditionalist," she stated briskly. "I thought it best that we take this into consideration."

Sam narrowed his eyes as he pondered her approach. He couldn't agree less, but he nodded for her to continue.

"Reed Sugar has been around for generations. It's a household name." Lila opened a folder and pulled out some vintage ads. "Why not appeal to the nostalgia?"

Sam stared at her. This would never do. "That's hardly sexy."

"It's sugar," Lila replied.

"Honey, I can make a potato look sexy." He roamed his gaze over her face. Her lips were pouted, full and pink, and he had a sudden urge to lean in, to taste her again, to show her just how good she made him feel.

Her gaze turned hooded. "I'm sure you can."

Lila folded her arms across her chest. Sam noticed the way the thin silk of her pink blouse shaped her round breasts. Her long legs were crossed, and a generous slit up her tight navy skirt sent a rush of heat straight to his groin. He rubbed his face to shake the image. Business first. Pleasure . . . *Don't go there, Sam.*

"Reed Sugar has been around forever, I agree, but when a company has been in business as long as they have, there's always the chance that they'll become a little . . . stale." Sam paused. "When people go to the grocery store, we don't want to give them the impression that they're buying their grandmother's brand—"

"Why not?" Lila challenged. "When a young mother

goes to the grocery store, don't you think she wants to give her children the trusted brand she has grown up with herself? It's a safe choice."

"Safe?" Sam guffawed.

"Yes, *safe*," Lila said. "Trustworthy. Solid."

"It's not my style to play it safe, Lila," Sam replied.

"No, and solid and trustworthy aren't adjectives I'd associate with you, either."

He chose not to react to that remark, but the implication stung just the same. Of course she'd assume that of him, and why shouldn't she? But he knew better than her that he was loyal. He just hadn't been able to be loyal to her. "For lack of a better word, Lila, it's just not cool."

"Not *cool?*" Lila erupted into laughter, a contagious peal laced with a bitter undertone.

Sam forced his tone to remain steady. "Yes, that's right. Not cool. Consumers want something current, fresh, and new. Everyone appreciates a classic car, but they're buying a brand new Mercedes."

"Well, how do you propose we attract new buyers without losing the ones we have?"

"Easy. We show them that sugar is a better choice than all those sweeteners that are popping up every year. It's not the *safe* choice. It's the *natural* choice." Sam grinned. It was the perfect tagline.

"Mitch isn't going to agree." Lila shook her head and flipped through her notes. As she bent forward, a hint of a black lace bra was revealed through the opening of her blouse. Sam cleared his throat.

"Oh, I think he will."

Lila's eyes widened in fury. "Well, *I* don't agree. Reed Sugar has been in business for seventy-five years. They're an American staple."

"And a thing of the past, Lila! Our goal is to keep Reed in business for another seventy-five years. They've got a lead on the sugar industry; that's not their competition. They want some sex appeal. They want something new."

"They could have just brought you in, and they didn't. They have hometown roots, they're traditionalists, and they want me to balance things out. I know how you and Rex operate. Big splash. Big money. Well, this is a collaborative effort and let's get one thing straight: you are *not* my boss. We will work together on this or we won't work on it at all."

"Taking yourself out of the running, then?"

"Quite the opposite," Lila fumed. "You're digging your own grave on this one, Sam. And I don't intend to go down with you."

To control his growing temper, he lowered his voice and chose his next words carefully. "We are going to work on this account, Lila, and I will not have you sabotage it for me. Is that understood?"

Lila met Sam's eyes for a brief second. "I think we've accomplished enough for one day." She stood and pushed her chair away from the desk with the back of her calves, giving him a full view of those endless legs and that perfect curve of her hips.

"I wouldn't say we've accomplished anything," he countered, rising.

Lila set her hands on her hips. "Do you have a compulsive need to disagree with everything I say?"

Sam stared her down until the fire in her eyes was snuffed. "We have a tight deadline and I'm not in town to sightsee. I'll be working on the pitch tonight. If you would like to be included, I'll expect to see you this evening after work. I'm staying at The Peninsula."

"But—"

Sam turned on his heel and flung open the door. "Seven o'clock," he said without turning back.

He smiled at the slack-jawed assistant and pushed through the front door, a rush of adrenaline hitting him as hard as the summer heat. If there was one thing that always put a little kick in his step, it was a good challenge. That, and the thought of seeing Lila again.

Chapter Five

The timer on the oven rang just as Lila was brushing her hair into a ponytail. She hurried into the kitchen, pulled on the oversized oven mitts that had once belonged to her grandmother, and opened the oven door. Warm cinnamon and sugar wafted through the air, and despite the trials of the day, Lila closed her eyes for a moment and grinned.

Some people found other ways to alleviate stress, she supposed, but for her, there was nothing more therapeutic than tying on her apron strings, pulling out the canisters and mixing bowls, and creating something delicious. Many of her fondest memories took place in the kitchen—a small one, not much different than this—in the apartment she and Mary shared with their grandparents. The girls would fight over who got to lick the spoon until Gram produced a second one, and there was always a cold glass of milk to enjoy when the treat was ready. They'd sit at the square table near the window and talk about their day, and save a few cookies for Gramps after he closed the ice cream parlor for the night.

She frowned a little as she transferred the cookies to a cooling rack. She missed those days.

Before she could start wallowing, she jotted down a few more ideas for her meeting with Sam. She knew that she was on to something. She could practically see the ad now. It was good. She knew it was good. And she knew Reed would think so, too.

Now, to just convince Sam . . .

When her notes were in order, Lila slid into her flip-flops, grabbed her oversized tote that was bulging with files, and quickly placed the cookies in a plastic container. They looked warm and gooey and smelled like heaven.

She smiled to herself. Sam didn't stand a chance.

*

Twenty minutes later, Lila stood in front of the six-panel mahogany door of Sam's suite. She was ten minutes late—something that ticked her off immensely. The last thing she needed was to be giving Sam any reason to doubt her ability, the way he was so quick to do in the past.

Balancing the cookies in one hand, she hovered her fist over the polished surface and finally tapped her knuckles three crisp times, the gesture exuding much more control over the situation than she felt.

She finally sensed a shuffling from the other side of the wall, and her breath caught as the lock turned and the door swung open. Sam was dressed casually in a gray T-shirt and well-worn jeans. He smelled of fresh aftershave and his dark, wavy hair was slightly wet; the combination immediately conjured images that Lila knew better than to embrace.

She tightened her grip on the container of cookies. This was going to be more difficult than she had hoped.

His lips parted into a pleased grin. "Well, hello. I wasn't sure if you'd be coming tonight."

Lila bit back a fresh wave of fury, all at once remembering the person she was dealing with here. "Hello, Sam," she said coolly.

He held his arm wide, welcoming her in, and she strode past him to a large sitting area. Floor-to-ceiling windows offered a corner view of an illuminated city skyline and, beyond it, Lake Michigan. Two oversized sofas and a pair of leather club chairs framed a square coffee table. At the opposite end was a dining table for six and a fully stocked wet bar with a mirrored backsplash. The room was larger than Lila's apartment, and judging from the multiple closed doors off a side hall, she could only assume there was even more to its grandeur. It was very flashy. Very . . . Sam.

"Impressive." She supposed to him it was just normal. Sam had grown up in luxury; he was accustomed to the finer things in life. He had come to expect nothing but the best, and probably swept his eyes over this place with an impassive shrug. For not the first time, Lila was reminded of how different they were, of their conflicting values and experiences. Sam wouldn't have any idea what it would be like to spend a cold night nestled under a pile of blankets, giggling when her feet skimmed her sister's icy toes because the heat bill was too high that month, or to have to depend on a full scholarship for any hope of a college education.

Sunshine Creamery had hardly allowed them a life of luxury, but what Sam would never understand is that it wasn't money that had mattered to them.

Lila crossed the room and set her things on the dining table. At the wet bar, Sam was already mixing a cocktail. He turned to her with a mischievous grin.

She felt her lips thin. He wasn't going to make this easy for her, was he?

"For you, *Madame*," Sam said gallantly, handing her a pink-hued martini.

"That would be *Mademoiselle*, actually," she corrected him. She flirted with the stem of her glass, unsure if she wanted to give in to the temptation. As if his mere presence wasn't difficult enough to resist, he had to go and sweeten the deal.

Shame on him for bribing his way on to her good side.

"Ah, well, I never could figure out that language." Sam took a sip of his own drink—scotch, his favorite—and wandered into the living area. He sat down on a sofa and tossed her a grin. "Come sit over here. It's more comfortable."

Lila sighed. If only she could keep her back to him. Anything to avoid looking at that face. Taking her drink and a few files and deliberately leaving the cookies where they were, she joined Sam around the large coffee table. Without meeting his eye for fear of wavering, she arranged herself on the sofa opposite his. He may have gotten her into his corner, but she would hardly make herself within arm's reach, even if deep down she would have loved nothing more than to sit close enough to see the curl of his black lashes and smell the musk of his freshly shampooed hair.

Stop it, Lila.

"I can order something for us to eat if you'd like."

He was being nice, she knew, but it was too late for that. Six years too late. Dinner together last night had been a mistake, and not one she could afford to repeat. On any level. There had been far too little progress with the account and far too much gazing into those blue eyes. "I'm here to work, not to eat."

"Suit yourself," Sam replied with a shrug.

Lila clicked the top of her pen. "Have you given any more consideration to my ideas?"

Sam arched an eyebrow. "Would it matter?"

"As a matter of fact, it would." Lila forced her voice to remain calm. "We're collaborating on this effort, after all."

Sam shrugged and his lips did a funny little dance. Lila choked back a surge of fury that threatened to explode. She could throw that martini right in that smug face . . . Forcing a deep breath, she reached a shaking hand for the glass and took a long sip of the fruity sweetness instead.

"Good?" Sam asked.

Lila licked her lips. "It did the trick."

Sam set his tumbler down on a marble coaster and leaned forward, resting his elbows on his knees. "I think it's fair to say that we don't exactly have the same vision for this campaign."

"I'll agree with you there."

A hint of a smile passed over Sam's face. He paused, his eyes roaming over her until she had to glance away. "Why don't we start over, Lila?" he asked.

"Start over?" she repeated. "I put a lot of thought into my ideas for this campaign, Sam. I know you don't agree with them, but if we could discuss our visions a bit more, I might be able to—"

Sam's mouth spread into a sad, thin-lipped smile. His brow set in a straight line. "I mean start over with us. You and me. Forget the past."

Lila scoffed, but her heart somersaulted. Something within the pit of her stomach knotted. Tightly.

"It's not that easy . . ." She grew quiet, her mind reeling when she thought of how badly he'd hurt her, the tears she'd cried for this man. She squirmed on the cushion and reached for her cocktail, finding she had suddenly lost the taste for it. She set it back on the table and heaved a long sigh, cursing herself for the sudden vulnerability she felt and couldn't hide. Showing weakness in front of Sam wasn't an option, and here she was, bordering on breaking the one promise to herself she intended to keep.

"No, I suppose it's not." Sam sighed heavily. "Can I get you another drink?" he asked, standing to stretch his strong frame. He glanced at her full glass and cast her a lopsided smile. "You always nursed those things. No wonder. They're too sweet for me."

A heaviness settled in her chest as she watched him cross the room. She let her eyes linger on his broad shoulders and the thick biceps that curved beneath the thin veil of his shirt. He might be an arrogant jerk, but she couldn't fight the attraction. And that was precisely why it was better for her to stay away. A man like Sam could only bring one thing to her life.

Handsome or not, he wasn't worth the heartache.

*

Sam studied Lila silently across the large coffee table as she reached up and pulled the band from her ponytail. Her chestnut hair spilled loosely over her shoulders, and she tucked one strand behind her ear, revealing the same pearl earrings she'd worn ever since he met her. She'd removed her shoes and sat curled up on the plush carpet with long, bare legs tucked delicately beneath the curve of her skirt. She was almost close enough to reach out and touch.

And it was taking everything in him not to do just that.

Back when he and Lila were dating, his mind was on one thing and one thing only, and that was rising to the top of his family's company. Six years later, he hadn't really changed much at all. He was sitting here with a stunning woman, and despite how much he wanted her, his mind was still wandering over to thoughts of the agency. And to thoughts of his father.

"You still wear those," he said, gesturing to her earlobe. He sucked in a breath, fighting the sudden urge to graze it with his teeth. "I wanted to buy you another pair for Christmas, and you told me not to, remember that?"

Lila's smile seemed a little sad. "My mother used to wear these . . . I used to beg her to let me wear them." She cleared her throat. "We should talk about business."

Sam nodded. He knew Lila had lost her parents—it was probably part of the reason he felt so connected to her. A woman like Lila could understand him, if he let her. Somehow, though, he could never bring himself to open up to her. It was too risky. There was too much at stake. Instead, he'd kept the wall up, just enough, careful to keep his head one step ahead of his heart.

Lila was right. He still had to focus on his mission for this evening. "Right. Back to business."

Lila's lips curved into a mysterious smile as she stood and crossed the room. He watched her with growing interest. The backs of her thighs were smooth and lithe, the slit of the skirt giving an enticing sneak peek into what lie beneath.

"I have a surprise for you," she said over her shoulder.

Sam pulled his eyes from her legs, watching in confusion as she strode toward him with what appeared to be nothing other than a plate full of cookies.

*

Lila wavered slightly, and then forced one foot in front of the other until she reached the sofa where Sam still sat.

Had he actually been checking her out? She knew she should have worn jeans, but it was too hot outside. Besides, the flip-flops were about as casual as she was willing to go, and that was mostly on account of her feet, which were still aching from those heels she'd worn for the lunch with Reed. She smoothed her pink blouse with one hand and proffered the plastic container with the other.

Sam stared at the cookies with a look of bewilderment. "What is this?"

"They're cookies." When he said nothing, she added, "I baked them. With Reed Sugar."

Sam groaned, but there was a curl at the corner of his mouth. "Nice play."

"Have one. They're snickerdoodles."

His hand stopped midair as he looked up at her. "*Snickerdoodles?*"

"That's what they're called. Didn't your mother ever

make them for you?"

Sam's expression darkened as he hastily took a cookie. "My mother didn't bake." He took a bite, chewing thoughtfully. "These are pretty good."

Lila fought back a pleased smile. "Thank you," she said. She set the container on the coffee table and resumed her spot on the opposite couch. Sam finished his cookie and reached for another one. Lila felt her pulse kick. This was it. "It makes you feel good, doesn't it? Eating that cookie? It takes you back to another time, a better time, back when you were a kid and—"

Sam squared his jaw. His stare was cold. "I told you. My mother didn't bake."

"No, but—" Lila sighed. This wasn't going as well as she had hoped. "Baking. Recipes. Childhood treats. It stirs up emotions. It makes you want to relive experiences. If we focus on that feeling of nostalgia, the ability to recreate a memory—"

"We're here to bounce ideas off one another, Lila. Not lock ourselves into one vision."

Sam finished his cookie and wiped his hands on his jeans. Before she knew what he was doing, he stood and came around the coffee table to sit down next to her. Despite herself, Lila felt her body stiffen with desire. She shifted to the end of the couch, but Sam didn't seem to notice. He rested his elbow on the back cushion, and tipped his head. "If you want me to go with this idea, you're going to have to sell me, and I'm not sold. Give me your pitch. Pretend I'm Reed."

Lila narrowed her gaze. "Don't talk down to me, Sam," she warned.

"I'm not talking down to you!" Sam's brow shot up in surprise. He looked so genuinely surprised at the insinuation that Lila felt a twinge of self-doubt.

But then, he was so used to getting his way, he didn't even realize when he was manipulating a situation anymore.

"I don't know how many times I have to remind you that you are not my boss. Not on this project. Not anywhere," Lila said icily. She worked independently for a reason—it meant her welfare was in her own hands, not someone else's. Certainly not Sam's.

Sam tipped his chin, his grin wry. "Don't mind me for stating the obvious here, Lila, but I think you're overreacting."

"Maybe I am. But for someone who is so hell-bent on putting their family above anyone else, I'm sort of surprised you're so quick to shut down my idea. But then, I guess that's nothing new."

Sam regarded her carefully. "Do you really want to get into this?"

It was a sobering question. Lila sat back, shaking her head. "It doesn't matter. What's done is done."

"But see, that's just it. You claim you've moved on. You take a chance every opportunity you have to tell me how far you've come, and yet you can't stop reminding me of the past. You're holding this over me, Lila, and that's not fair."

Well, that was rich. "There was nothing *fair* about what you did to me, Sam. Professionally or otherwise."

"I tried to help you," Sam protested.

"Help me?" Lila scoffed. "Sam, you kicked me off your campaign. That same day I got my pink slip. You sat in the room and said nothing in my defense as your father fired me. I waited for you to call . . ." She stopped herself. She'd said too much.

She chanced a glance in his direction, wondering just how much that little tidbit boosted his ego. Strangely, he looked more sad than pleased.

Lila swallowed hard and reached for her drink.

There was a side to Sam that would always be appealing. But the other side of him won out every time.

"When it comes to my family, it's complicated," Sam said. "I wish you could understand that."

She wasn't about to let him off the hook that easily. "I do see that. I see someone who is so determined to get to the top and stay at the top that they don't care who they knock down in the pursuit. You have no trouble going after what you want and trampling over everyone in your path to get there. No apology. No responsibility. It's all about money to you. All about getting ahead in your family business."

Silence stretched louder than any of the words she had just spoken. "Maybe you're right," Sam said eventually, and Lila was jarred by his calm, even tone.

She hadn't been expecting that.

Realizing she alone was fighting this battle, she swallowed quickly and waited for the heat to fade from her cheeks. If there was anyone in this world who brought out the worst in her, it was the man sitting next to her.

She really needed to get away from him.

She began scrambling for her belongings, clumsily stacking her paperwork and accidentally dropping her pen. It rolled to Sam's feet, and he bent to reach it.

"Here." His smooth voice was dangerously deep as she took the pen from his hand. The quick touch of his fingers sent a shock of electricity down her spine that tingled long after she had pulled away.

"You can keep the cookies," she managed, as she hurried to the door, sensing him close behind. With her hand on the knob, she turned abruptly, her heart sinking at the sight of him just a few feet away.

Without the suit and tie, he looked like her old boyfriend, not like the coldhearted businessman who would do anything to stay on top. Sam. Just Sam. Sam who would wrap his thick arms around her and hold her all night long. Sam who would breathe into her hair, and kiss her neck, and who took her to a different sushi restaurant every Friday, just for fun. Sam who knew she liked fruity pink drinks and pearl earrings.

Sam who knew just what they'd shared and just what he'd ruined.

She straightened her spine.

"I have to go," she said again, more to herself than to him. She pulled open the door and walked out into the hall, this time without looking back.

Chapter Six

Since moving back to Chicago, Lila and Mary had resumed their weekly summer tradition of strolling through the neighborhood farmers market, making a picnic lunch from all their findings, and spending the afternoon at the beach sprawled out on their grandmother's old patchwork quilt, reading novels and fashion magazines. Since Mary had started taking shifts at a restaurant last month to save up a little extra money for the ice cream parlor, the second half of this cherished routine had been sacrificed. It was worth it, though. Just like suffering through another ten days with Sam would be worth it.

The day was warm, and the crowds were already thick on the section of Lincoln Park roped off for the market. Lila hitched her canvas tote higher on her shoulder and followed Mary to the flower stand—always their first stop of the day, even though they rarely treated themselves to anything more than the occasional bunch of sunflowers to cheer up their small kitchen table.

"I have to be at work in an hour," Mary sighed. "I know I shouldn't complain, but there's a Cubs game today, and I just know it's going to get rowdy."

"Maybe you'll make some good tips," Lila said.

"Maybe." Mary brightened, as she always did when she started to think about the ice cream parlor. "Well, at least I'm off tomorrow. I'm going to spend the day at Sunshine. I need to perfect those waffle cones. I never could do it quite like Gramps . . ."

"He was one of a kind," Lila said wistfully.

Mary picked up a bouquet of pale pink roses, smelled them, and then set them back in a bucket. "You can come with me, if you'd like. Unless you have another date with Sam." She winked.

Lila was beginning to feel uneasy with all this talk of Sam and the ice cream parlor. It was taking everything in her not to tell Mary exactly the reason behind all her meetings with her ex-boyfriend. He'd left her alone for most of yesterday, at least, offering only a brief voice mail message that he had some other business to attend to, and an unsettling reminder that they both had a lot at stake. If only he knew just how much she had at stake . . .

Lila felt her lips thin. He probably wouldn't care. He certainly wouldn't understand why she was doing all this to save an ice cream parlor that had never turned much more than a bare bones profit.

Oh, Gramps. Lila couldn't fault him. How could her heart ever be filled with anything but love when she thought of the gleam in his eye when he came up with a new flavor, the ear to ear smile he'd flash when he handed her a triple cone? He was in the business of making people happy. Not getting rich. He'd passed the same sentiments down to his beloved granddaughters, teaching them through his actions more than his words that it was people he valued. Family, not money.

"Rain check?" Lila asked her sister. "I think I'll get a head start on the work week tomorrow." She had some other clients to attend to, and it would be better than worrying all day about how she was going to handle her next interaction with Sam, or how on earth they would possibly ever come to an agreement on this project.

"Only ten days until your next meeting with Reed Sugar!" Mary reminded her giddily. As if Lila hadn't been thinking the same thought since the moment she'd opened her eyes this morning. Well, that and how good Sam looked in a T-shirt. "Why do you look so worried? You have a huge client roster."

But none as big as Reed Sugar.

The girls walked over to the next stand, where they loaded their bags with fresh blueberries.

"Remember that blueberry cheesecake ice cream Gramps used to make?" Mary asked, grinning.

"He only used fresh berries." Lila smiled, thinking of

how every summer he'd bring them down to Michigan, hand them each a bucket, and tell them to pick as many berries as they could. "You would eat more off the bush than you'd collect in your pail."

Mary laughed. "I'm planning to bring that flavor back, only I might add my own touch with a bit of graham cracker crust mixed in."

Lila tried to look as enthusiastic as her sister, but she couldn't help worrying. They'd agreed to wait six months before selling the storefront, until the end of summer. It was unlikely another account as big as Reed would come along before then, if ever. Nothing was a sure thing yet. And if Lila had learned anything from her time with Sam, it was that nothing ever was.

"Lila? Lila?"

Lila blinked quickly and looked at her sister, who could only laugh at her confusion. "Boy, you do have a lot on your mind these days. You didn't even notice that your phone is ringing."

Lila frowned, suddenly hearing the electronic jingle. She pulled the phone from her back pocket and glanced at the screen, her breath catching when she noticed the name on the screen. All these years later, she still hadn't deleted the contact. What was she holding on to? Some fantasy that Sam would stumble back into her life?

Sadly, she knew the answer to that. The few dates she'd been on in Chicago had been disappointing. No one could excite her like Sam.

And no one, she'd promised herself, could hurt her like him either.

"Hello?" She turned away so her sister wouldn't overhear anything that might be said.

"What are you doing?" Sam asked, ignoring small talk altogether.

Lila paused, trying to understand what he was implying. "You mean . . . now?"

"Meet me at Belmont Harbor at noon," Sam said.

"I—"

But he cut her off before she could think of an excuse quickly enough.

"It was Sam, wasn't it?" Mary asked as Lila pushed her phone back into her pocket. "That makes three dates in one week!"

"It's a business meeting," she said to Mary, but she couldn't meet her sister's eye, because this time, she wasn't so sure that's all it was.

*

Sam had been waiting on the dock for twenty minutes when Lila finally appeared. She'd shed the uptight corporate look, he noticed with an appreciative grin, not that he minded the tight skirts that grazed her knees and hugged her curves. As she walked toward him, he allowed himself a moment to take in the flare of her hips under tight navy capri pants, and the swell of her breasts under her thin white tank top.

Sunglasses hid her eyes, but from the pout of her lips,

he could only assume they were burning with accusation.

"What is this?" she demanded, folding her arms across her chest as she came to a stop a safe five feet from where he was leaning against the sailboat he'd rented for the afternoon.

"A little thing called team work," Sam replied. "Have you sailed before?"

Lila tipped her chin. She didn't look amused.

"It's a two-person job," he continued.

"How do you know I don't get seasick?" Lila inquired.

Sam frowned. He hadn't factored that into his plan. "Do you?"

Lila sighed. "No."

"Then you don't have an excuse." He held out his hand, but she brushed past him and climbed onto the boat. She struggled slightly, losing her balance at one point, and leaned on the wheel to steady herself, but Sam knew better than to press his offer to help.

He stood back, admiring the way the sun caught the highlights in her hair and brought out a hint of pink in her bare shoulders, swallowing his smile as she finally took her seat, her nose slightly lifted, her profile proud. Without any more hesitation, he began untying the bow line.

Lila watched all this in silence. "Do you know what you're doing?" she asked warily.

Sam grinned. "I told you. My dad has a boat at his beach house. We do this every summer. Spend a day on the water, have some food, some drinks . . ." Only it wasn't as idyllic as he was making it out to be. It was more the way he wished it could be. The boating afternoons often consisted of business talk—clients, staff, money, competition. He longed for something deeper, for a few belly laughs even. But he'd settle for what he had. It was more than he'd expected at one point in time, after all. "Help yourself to some water if you want—there's a cooler near your feet."

Lila didn't move. "What is this, Sam?"

"I told you," he said, tossing the rope to the side. "Team work. If we're gonna win that account, we need to learn to lean on each other. Besides, once I have you out on the water, you can't exactly run off and leave again."

"I can swim," Lila said.

"Honey, do you know how cold that water is?" Sam laughed as he stepped into the boat. "Here. I'm going to turn on the motor, and you're going to help steer us out of the slip while I manage the spring line."

Lila looked alarmed. "But I've never driven a boat before."

"You'll do great," Sam said, motioning to the wheel. He started the engine and listened to its steady purr. "Let the engine warm up while I cast off the stern line. I'll tell you when I'm ready." Before she could protest, he untied the ropes and maneuvered the spring line around the dock post. "We're near the end of the fairway, so all we want to do is bring it forward and then take it to the left. Ready?"

Her knuckles were white as she gripped the wheel, but they were moving slowly, and he knew in a pinch he could jump down and take the helm. "Great. A little more to the left. That's it." Once they left the slip, he waited to see if she'd ask him to take over, but she surprised him by taking his direction instead.

She was starting to trust him again. At least he hoped she was.

"Now it's time raise the main sail," Sam grinned. "First thing we need to do is point the boat into the wind." He came up behind her and set his hands on either side of the wheel, pressing his chest against her back. Her hair was blowing in the breeze, tickling his face, but he took his time turning, wanting to hold on to the moment.

Beneath him, Lila felt warm and small. His arms brushed against hers, sending a jolt straight to his groin, and he leaned in a little closer. "See, just like this."

He glanced down at her neck, so smooth and long, wanting more than anything to bury his face in the little crook where it met her shoulder, to trace a path with his mouth, up, up, until his lips were on hers.

Stiffening, he pulled back. He squinted against the sun and began releasing the boom vang. He didn't look at Lila again until the sail was raised and they were moving steadily.

"You're good at this," Lila admitted with a slow smile, leaving the helm to sit on the edge of the boat beside him. "Did you always sail?"

Sam pulled a bottle of water out of the cooler and twisted the cap. "Nope," he said. "I picked it up when I was in college." He glanced at her sidelong, but she didn't seem suspicious.

Leaning back into her palms, she smiled up at the sky. They were headed south, and as the skyline came into better view, Lila pointed out a few of the buildings. They were keeping things light, making an effort, he supposed, but eventually they had to get around to discussing Reed. He'd spent most of yesterday fielding calls from the agency, trying to deal with the crisis unfolding. It felt good to forget about that for a while.

"My parents took us boating once," Lila offered. "It was just a canoe, but my sister and I loved it."

Sam waited for her to go on, but that seemed to be all she wanted to share. She'd told him about her parents early into their relationship, matter-of-factly, the way one could only do about something that had happened a long time ago but still hurt to this day. There was an expectation that eventually you got over those types of things, that the pain faded, and you moved on. He saw the hurt in her eyes, the way she dismissed the subject just as quickly as she'd broached it with a shrug of her shoulders and a brave smile that drooped at the corners. It tore something open inside him—a wound he'd never let heal. He wanted to tell her he got it, he understood, but instead he'd squeezed her hand, taken a swig of his drink, followed her lead, and switched topics.

"It was one of the last memories I have of them," Lila

whispered, almost to herself.

Sam ground down on his teeth. "You're lucky to have that."

She gave him a little half smile. "You're father wasn't interested in canoe trips when you were little?"

Sam shrugged. He wouldn't know, would he? "My father's life was that company. It still is," he said tightly.

"I was surprised to hear he'd retired," Lila commented.

Sam stiffened. To the public they'd made it appear that Preston has stepped down by his own free will. No one knew about the early onset Alzheimer's that eventually made it impossible for him to oversee the company.

"Oh, he still keeps his toe in the water," Sam said gruffly, forcing back the emotions that hit him full force. It happened every time he thought of the bitter irony of his situation. Only when he finally found his father did he stand to lose him again. Oh, the man was still sharp, still a bigger than life force, but every now and then Sam was reminded . . . time was running out. He had to make the most of this opportunity with his father. Had to make him proud while he still could. "My dad is a tough man to please."

Lila just raised an eyebrow. "Easy for you to say."

"No." Sam shook his head, his laugh a little brittle. "Not easy for me." He studied Lila's profile for a long time: the slight turn of her nose, the pouty lips, and the little curve of her chin—waiting for her to turn and look at him. She didn't.

He closed his eyes, feeling that weight in his chest again. The one he felt every time he thought of that day his father had fired her. He'd told his dad it was a mistake, that Lila was smart, clever and witty, but Preston Crawford had looked bored and then angry. No one disagreed with Preston. Certainly not Sam.

"Lila, I want to tell you . . . I'm sorry, Lila." There. It was out. Fat load of good it would do him now, but it was out. Maybe it made him look like a coward, maybe it made him look like an ass. But he was sorry. More sorry than she'd ever know.

He pushed back the burning urge to explain everything to her, and then thought twice. It had grown too easy to keep his past locked up, until he barely thought about it himself anymore. It was easier that way.

For a moment he wondered if she'd even heard him. Her eyes were still on the buildings in the distance. Her expression didn't move an inch. With a sigh, she pushed her sunglasses on top of her head. Her hazel eyes were crinkled slightly at the corners when she turned to him. With the sun on her face, she'd never looked more beautiful.

"I didn't handle things well," Sam continued. The need for release was stronger than the need to keep up the walls. "I wanted to run after you. I wanted to be with you. I didn't know how I could."

"Because of your father," she finished. She didn't look impressed.

Sam pulled in a breath and nodded. "Besides, would

you really have wanted to still be with me?"

Lila considered this for a long moment. "I guess not. I guess to me it was all connected. One event. When you betrayed me."

Ouch. Sam folded his arms over his knees and looked away. He probably deserved that one.

"Your business means a lot to you," Lila said.

"My *family* means a lot to me," he corrected.

Lila held his gaze for a moment and finally tipped her head. "So does mine. I guess it's why we do what we do."

She had that right. From the moment he'd discovered that Preston Crawford was his father, he'd made it his mission to set himself up for success. To be the son his dad would be proud of. If there had never been a Preston Crawford, or if he was something other than the man he was, Sam wasn't sure what would have become of himself. He'd been on this path for so long, he wasn't even sure what else was out there. Or what he'd given up.

He looked at Lila. Make that who he'd given up.

They had the boat for another two hours, but Sam didn't feel like talking about Reed today. He rarely snagged a day off like this in New York—there were too many dinner meetings, golf outings, social obligations.

He reached into the cooler and pulled out a can of beer, wiggling his eyebrows at Lila by way of invitation. She laughed, then darted her eyes over the vast lake. "Are we—are you allowed?"

Now it was Sam's turn to laugh. "Don't see why not.

You want one?"

She made a little face, just as he'd expected. "Here." He reached into the cooler again and this time pulled out a wine cooler. She was the only person he knew who drank those damn things, and God, a part of him loved her for it.

She grinned, showing a hint of a dimple in her right cheek. "Thanks."

After a few sips, Lila repositioned herself on the deck. "So, now what do we do?"

"We wait."

"Wait?"

Sam shrugged. "For you to start liking me again."

Lila opened her mouth as if she had something to say and then closed it. Her eyes were soft as they locked his, the light bringing out flecks of gold around her pupils, and her lips were parted in a way that made every nerve ending in his body stand at attention. Her bare leg skimmed his knee, and even though it was probably involuntary, his pulse kicked up a notch. He set his beer down and inched his hand onto hers, up her warm skin, until he was cupping her neck, his fingers laced in her mess of hair that had grown tangled in the wind.

Alarm flickered through her gaze, and he heard her breath catch as he leaned in, slowly, eager to taste her sweetness, to feel the heat of her body. Her mouth was inches from his, and he could see her lashes flutter. "Sam."

He stopped himself right there.

"Sorry," he said, picking up the beer and taking a long drink. "Went to my head." He grinned, knowing she didn't buy his lame excuse any more than he did. He wanted to kiss her, wanted to lean her back and press himself on top of her, hear her moan his name in his ear, not push it out like some sort of warning.

But he couldn't. More than six years may have passed since they'd last seen each other, but nothing had changed. She was still Lila. Sweet, beautiful Lila. And he was still Preston Crawford's son. The person he'd always wanted to be.

Except when he was with Lila.

Chapter Seven

Lila brushed her fingers over her lips, wondering what might have happened if she hadn't spoiled the moment. He'd been about to kiss her—there was no doubt about it—but why?

She hardly dared to entertain the thought that he might still have feelings for her after all this time. It had been six years. Who held on to the past for that long?

Lila pulled a mug from the kitchen cabinet and set it firmly on the counter. *Guilty as charged.*

She stared out the window above the sink as the coffee percolated, looking out at the stately row of townhomes tucked neatly behind wrought iron fences. She knew few of her neighbors—people tended to offer little more than a passing nod when they crossed each other on the sidewalks—but she loved their apartment, just a few blocks from the park, and a short walk from her office. Mary and Lila always joked that even once they were married, they'd stay on their happy little tree-lined street, and grow competing herb gardens on their fire escapes.

With each passing year, though, it was starting to feel like *if* they got married.

"Ugh, I do not want to go to work today," Mary groaned as she stumbled into the kitchen, barefoot and still in her striped cotton pajamas. She walked straight to the cupboard, took out a mug, and poured herself a cup of coffee, even though the pot was only partially full. "You know, he winked at me on Friday. As he passed my desk for lunch. The creep."

Lila had to laugh, and eventually Mary joined in. Her boss was a sixty-year-old ear, nose, and throat specialist with a wife who did the books and was forever nagging him about watching his cholesterol. The bickering was fierce, and neither seemed to care that Mary heard every word. Lila had told her sister early on that she was probably the bright spot in the poor man's day. Still, Mary wanted out, and Lila could hardly blame her.

"I could barely sleep last night, Lila." Mary leaned back on the counter and blew on her coffee.

"Oh, he's harmless—"

"Not about that! And you're right, he is harmless. Annoying and sad, but harmless. No, I couldn't stop thinking about the ice cream parlor! I came up with another fun flavor. Are you ready for it?" Her brown eyed danced with excitement.

Lila took her time filling her mug and adding a splash of milk. "I'm all ears."

"Oh!" Mary thwacked her arm. "That's what Dr. McTavish always says. He thinks it's the funniest thing ever, but I'm losing the will to laugh."

Lila grinned as she reached for the sugar bowl, but her hand froze on the spoon as nerves came fluttering back to the surface. It had been so nice to take the day off yesterday, to go into the quiet office and catch up on work, then clean the house and grocery shop, and not have to worry about Sunshine Creamery, Reed, or Sam. Of course, part of her had idly wondered all day if he might call, and okay, yes, at times she was admittedly hoping he would. But he hadn't, and really, that was for the best.

The last thing she needed was for him to try to kiss her again, right?

Lila looked down at the ceramic sugar bowl edged with chipped, painted blue flowers and felt her eyes sting. She'd seen this bowl many times before—and it was one of the few things she had to remember her grandparents by.

That and Sunshine Creamery.

She wondered if her mother had studied the little flowers the way she liked to, if it was part of her morning ritual, back when she was a little girl. She often wondered what her mother had been like as a child, and she used to ask Gram about her parents all the time. Now there would be no more insight into the people who had left her life. Their memories could no longer be shared—their stories had come to an end.

She couldn't let their legacy end, too.

She dumped the sugar into her mug and stirred quickly.

"Anyway, I was thinking not just strawberry ice cream, but strawberries and cream . . . Isn't that sweet? And I might do a whole line like that . . . peaches and cream, blueberries and cream. Oh. And I was thinking that we should dust off the old soda fountain. Who doesn't love a malt?"

Lila plucked two pieces of bread from the toaster and began buttering them. She hadn't thought of that old machine in ages—it had belonged to their great-grandfather, the founder of Sunshine Creamery.

"You're really stirring up the nostalgia," she commented as she slid into her usual chair near the window.

Mary joined her at the table. "Well, yes, but with a few modern touches, of course."

Modern touches. Lila chewed a corner of her toast thoughtfully. It was exactly what was missing from her pitch. She'd make some notes before her next meeting with Sam. It might be just the thing she needed to convince him her idea would work.

*

At eight thirty sharp, Sam pushed open the door of Lila's office. It was time to get back on track, put that little slip up on Saturday behind him. He'd spent most of yesterday on the phone with Rex, and anxiety stirred in his gut when he considered what this work week could bring. Jolt Coffee could make an announcement at any time, and then . . . He pushed back the thought.

"Well, *hello* there!" Penny exclaimed as a bright, wide smile transformed her round face. She tossed aside the fashion magazine she was reading and stood, quickly smoothing the creases from her flouncy, floral-patterned skirt.

Sam grinned. "Good morning, Penny."

Two pink dots appeared on her cheeks. "I didn't think you'd remember my name."

"I never forget a name," Sam said, deciding it was time to draw an end to this round of flirtation. There was only one woman on his mind today, and he certainly didn't need to stoke her temper this early into the morning. "I brought you something."

"Oh?"

Sam set a bottle of water on the desk. "Well, it's for Fred."

Penny laughed, a high-pitched giggle that she struggled to suppress. Sam waited until she had calmed down before explaining, "I'm actually here to see Lila. Is she in yet?"

Disappointment wrinkled Penny's brow. "Not yet."

Huh. Not what Sam had been expecting to hear.

"Mind if I wait for her?"

"Certainly." Penny nodded toward a waiting room chair.

Sam flashed a hundred-watt grin and cocked his head. "Mind if I wait for her in her office instead? I'm on a tight schedule and I'd love to set up my materials."

Penny glanced worriedly at the front door. "Well . . ."

"Penny? Is that by any chance short for Penelope?" Sam asked, giving her another well-mastered grin.

"It is," she said warily.

"That's one of my favorite names, believe it or not."

Penny lowered her eyes as her cheeks turned a brighter shade of pink. "I'd like to help you out, but . . ."

"You know guys like me. I've got so much on my plate, and if I can save five minutes by setting things up in advance . . ." He lowered his voice to a conspiratorial whisper. "It would really help me out a lot, Penelope." He let the last word roll of his tongue.

"Okay . . . but if I get in trouble . . ."

Sam fought back a satisfied grin and held both palms up defensively. "I'll take the fall."

Penny flashed one last smile and motioned to the French doors to her right. "Go ahead."

Sam nodded his thanks and slipped through the door. Flicking on the light switch, he glanced around the room, taking a better look around this time. It was very . . . Lila. Neat and clean and feminine. A small paperclip holder. A stack of pens arranged by color. A flurry of Post-it note reminders framing a corkboard. A white desk against the soothing green walls. A framed print of red tulips. A cuckoo clock. He paused. Now, that he hadn't expected.

His eyes darted to the half-open door before quickly shifting back to the calendar on her desk. Finding nothing of interest there, he turned to a well-organized file system on the edge of her desk. He stole another look in the direction of the waiting room before plucking a folder from its rack and riffling through the pages as fast as his fingers would let him.

"What the *hell* are you doing?"

Sam glanced up guiltily to see Lila standing in the doorway, looking every bit as sexy as she had on Saturday. He raked his eyes over her figure, from her bare ankles all the way up to her clenched jaw and narrowed eyes.

"Something tells me you aren't happy to see me," he ventured, attempting to lighten the situation.

She closed the door firmly behind her. "For once I'm happy to say that you're right."

"Touché," he said, coming around the desk.

"It looks like I'll have to have a chat with my assistant," she said, taking the file from his hands and sitting down at her desk. "I didn't expect to see you this morning."

"I'm an early riser," Sam said, taking one of the visitor's chairs. "I would have called first, but—"

She lifted an eyebrow. "But?"

She wasn't going to make this easy on him. "I wasn't

so sure you'd take the call."

Her lips twisted with amusement. "You know me too well."

"I know you very well." He held her gaze until her smile fell.

She pinched her lips and straightened a pile of papers against the desk; the sound cut the silence but did little for the tension.

Why couldn't he have let it go? Why couldn't he just keep his eye on the goal?

He allowed his gaze to passively roam over her. It seemed impossible that this was the same woman he had almost kissed just two days ago. The loose tendrils of chestnut locks that had caught the wind off the sails were now pulled back in a severe knot. Her full, cherry-hued lips were now pursed tight in defiance. And her eyes, which had held his so seductively, were now set in stone.

She was watching him down the length of her perfectly little upturned nose, her arms now folded tightly against her chest. Those pouty lips remained pursed, just begging to be kissed, and it was taking everything in him not to jump out of his chair, lean over the desk, and close the distance between them.

He'd tried to resist the feeling all those years ago, knowing better than to mix his personal life with his professional one, but he hadn't been able to. And now, all these years later, he still couldn't fight the way she made him feel when she laughed, the way his groin tightened when she was near, the way he didn't want to be with anyone else when he was with her.

He'd let her go once. He didn't want to make the same mistake twice. Looking at her closely, Sam decided that he now had two missions to accomplish during his stay in Chicago.

He would land the Reed Sugar campaign. And he would win back Lila Harris. Somehow.

*

Lila let her eyes skim through the pages of the Reed Sugar folder once more, grateful for the chance to stall and think. Nothing appeared to be missing at first glance, but she wouldn't have expected Sam to have pocketed any of these papers. He might have stolen her heart, but he wasn't an actual thief.

She glanced at him, her mouth a thin line of disapproval, but the sight of his guilty, boyish grin caused her heart to flip over.

She really had to stop doing this. Her attraction had interfered with her ambition once before, clouding her judgment, leading to her demise. It couldn't happen again.

She drew a breath. "So—"

At the sound of her voice, Sam mildly cocked an eyebrow. His eyes darkened with interest, pulling her in, causing her to lose her train of thought. A quiver that began at the base of her spine chased its way up to the roots of Lila's hair. Involuntarily, she shivered.

Silence stretched as she waited for him to speak, and

she swallowed hard, wondering where to even begin. If he would mention the almost kiss, if she should pretend it meant nothing. Because that's exactly what it had to mean: nothing.

"Is there something we needed to talk about?" She instantly regretted the words as they spilled from her mouth.

"I was hoping we could make some progress on the campaign," Sam said with an affable shrug of his broad shoulders, and a fresh surge of confusion rolled through Lila's chest.

"Right now?" she asked.

"Do you have a better idea?"

"Actually, I have many good ideas. If you would bother listening to them," she added.

Sam chuckled softly, the rumble building to a roar of laughter.

"What's so funny?" Lila snapped.

"You are," Sam said, a lazy grin lingering on his face as he rubbed the back of his neck. "You never change, Lila. It's . . . it's so refreshing." His blue eyes flashed, and Lila pinched her lips.

She struggled to digest his words, not knowing whether to take them as a compliment or an insult. Or an accusation.

She decided to brush it aside. They had work to do—lots of work—and they had already wasted enough time as it was. Clearly the almost kiss was already forgotten by

Sam, and the last thing she intended to do was feed that enormous ego of his and ask him to reassure her or clarify. It happened. And now it was over. And it would never happen again.

And she was a fool to be feeling the twinge of hurt creeping over her heart at that thought.

Lila tapped a stack of papers on her desk sharply until the edges lined up and gave Sam another long, hard stare from under the hood of her lashes. "Let's begin, then."

"Have you reconsidered my angle?" Sam leaned back in his chair and folded his arms across his chest.

"No, I most certainly have not!" Lila stated boldly. "Have you reconsidered mine?"

Sam shrugged. "Nope."

To think she had almost kissed this jerk! "Well, then." Lila cast him a withering stare and then lowered her eyes. This was turning into a disaster. "I had another thought this morning . . ."

"If it involves cookies and baking, I don't want to hear it."

Lila pressed a finger against her forehead and took a deep breath. "What's going to happen if we don't come to an agreement?"

She glanced at Sam out of the corner of her eye and saw that he looked just as worried as she felt. "Maybe we need to have a talk with Reed. Tell them this isn't working."

"And run the risk of them taking their business elsewhere? There are plenty of big advertising agencies in

Chicago," Lila pointed out. Ones that would go head to head with Sam, not collaborate with him.

Lila bit down on her thumbnail. The history she had with Jeremy Reed had helped her case, but what about Sam? Why would an agency like his bow to a potential client's demands?

She was just about to ask Sam that exact question, when his phone began to vibrate.

He frowned when he looked at the screen. "I have to take this. We'll finish this conversation later."

"When?" The meeting was next Wednesday, and she felt more panicked now than she had at last week's lunch.

"Whenever you're ready to drop that stale idea," Sam said. With a push of a button, he connected the call. "Hello?" Glancing to meet Lila's outraged stare, he casually held up his free hand by way of a good-bye and opened the door.

Lila sat perfectly still as the sound of his voice faded and the front door closed behind him. Of all—

"Argh!" Lila gave her palm a satisfying *whack* on the cold, hard surface of her desk. She swiveled her chair to face the window, her heart pounding. Hot tears sprung to her eyes and quickly blurred her vision of the tree-lined street as Sam appeared on the sidewalk. She blinked twice and wiped away the evidence of with the edge of her pointer finger.

No more tears. Not for that man.

She would have thought by now she'd be over him.

But in the six days since Sam had come back into her life, all those original, raw emotions had resurfaced. It was becoming too much.

And she had another eight days of this to go.

Seeing him today had done nothing to make her feel better about that near miss on Saturday. Had it been so meaningless to him that it wasn't even worth mentioning? Had he regretted it? Forgotten it? Or was it a tactic to get her on his good side, to smooth talk her into giving him his way?

Lila simply had no idea. But one thing was very clear.

She was over Sam Crawford.

Chapter Eight

Sam closed his notebook and slid it back into his briefcase just as the cab swerved to a stop in front of his hotel. Rumors about Jolt Coffee were starting to spread, and the pressure to land Reed Sugar was building. Account executives were diffusing the situation by making lunches, assuring their clients that nothing was wrong, doing damage control to ensure no one got the same idea and took their business elsewhere.

It wasn't lost on the brothers that since their father had stepped down last fall, clients were nervous.

"It's perfect timing, really," Rex was saying. "We overshadow the bad news with the good. No one will care that we lost Jolt when we land Reed."

"Dad will care," Sam said.

"Hey, it's the best chance we have to soften the blow,"

Rex replied. "So don't ruin it."

"I told you, it's under control," Sam said, even though nothing could be further from the truth.

"Before I let you go, there's something else you should know," Rex said.

Sam pushed through the lobby doors and set his bag down on a table. He knew what was coming, but somehow it never got any easier. "What happened?"

Rex waited a beat. "He locked himself out of the house again."

Sam closed his eyes. It still shocked him that such a powerful man could be subject to human struggles. He'd thought this father was invincible. Unbreakable. And oh, how he'd tried to break him. Tried to tear down the walls and get to the heart of the man. Tried to look past the obvious and search for something deeper. "Where were the keys this time?"

"In his pocket." Rex sighed. The last time this had happened, less than a month ago, the keys were in the mailbox, along with the letters he hadn't remembered to collect. "It was worse this time, Sam," Rex eventually said, and Sam felt his brows pinch.

"How so?"

"He didn't call anyone for help. I just happened to go over, and there he was, sitting on one of the garden chairs. In the rain. God only knows how long he'd been out there."

Sam sat down in the nearest chair and rubbed his forehead. Their father could go for days at a time without any setbacks; each time something like this occurred it was a fresh blow and a bitter reminder that no matter how much they wished it was wasn't happening, it was. They were losing him, ever so slowly, and Sam couldn't help feeling he'd only just found him.

"Where was the housekeeper?"

"In the kitchen, preparing dinner. I fired her. The new one started this morning."

Sam pulled in a long breath and released it slowly. Miranda had been hired to take care of the house and keep an eye on their father when the family couldn't be there, but this type of thing could have happened to anyone. It was just another example of the impossible standard the Crawfords held.

Sam should know. He was still trying to live up to it himself.

*

Mary was already home when Lila stepped into the apartment that evening. "Out here!" her sister called from the fire escape. "And grab the corkscrew on your way!"

Lila dropped her bag to the floor and wandered into the kitchen, where she retrieved the corkscrew from the utensil drawer. The apartment was warm and sticky, but the breeze filtering in through the screen door was cool on her skin. Feeling a little better, she opened the freezer and pulled out a container of cookie dough ice cream, grabbed two spoons, and stepped outside.

Mary grinned as she eyed the ice cream, then began uncorking a bottle of wine she must have bought on her way home from work.

"Rough day?" Lila asked as Mary filled their glasses.

"Eh. The usual. He passed my desk to get some water from the cooler exactly nineteen times." The girls laughed. "If you must know, the real reason for the wine is that I was hoping it might loosen your lips. You've been awfully quiet about all these little meetings with Sam."

Lila nailed her sister with a look, but Mary's eyes just turned pleading. "Oh do tell, Lila. Please! Let me live vicariously!"

"There's nothing to tell." Lila reached for her wine glass.

"Well, there's more than I have to share. Do you even know what I did the other night while you were off with a gorgeous blast from the past?" Without waiting for Lila to respond, she heaved a dramatic sigh and took a long sip of her wine. "I hung out at the local hardware store."

"The hardware store?" Lila frowned. "Why?"

Mary widened her eyes. "To see if any eligible men wanted to show me where I could find the sandpaper," she said, throwing her head back in laughter. "I spent forty-five minutes wandering the aisles, surrounded by hammers and nails and all sorts of boring stuff, in a vain search for Mr. Right. So forgive me for hoping that your love life is a little more satisfying than mine."

Lila chuckled and handed her sister a spoon. "Ice

cream?"

Mary shrugged "Why not? Your little reunion with Sam Crawford is the most exciting thing to have happened in months, and I need a snack while I take in the entertainment."

Lila pinched her lips. "I told you—"

"I know, I know." Mary held up a hand. "But I still want to know everything."

Everything. Lila sighed, feeling her shoulders deflate.

"I told you these were just business meetings," she said carefully, noting the unconvinced arch of Mary's eyebrow. "And I meant that. Sam . . . Well, we're sort of working together on this pitch."

Mary's brow wrinkled with confusion. "The one for the sugar company?"

Lila nodded. She hated having to worry her sister, but misleading her felt far worse.

"Well, that's perfect!" Mary burst out happily. She dug her spoon into the ice cream and brought a scoop to her mouth. "Isn't he one of the best?"

"Yes," Lila said begrudgingly, thinking of that smug smirk, the swagger around the office, the hand casually folded into his pocket, the way women around him savored every flash of those perfect white teeth and men stood a little straighter when he crossed their path. Sam was the best. And he knew it, too.

"Then what do you have to worry about?" Mary asked. "If you're working with Sam, then there's no doubt you'll get the account. And you know what that means!" She clapped her hands together excitedly. "I was thinking of doing a triple-dipped waffle cone. Dark chocolate, milk chocolate, white chocolate. Don't you love it?"

Lila's smile felt grim. "Gramps would have loved it."

Mary topped off their glasses and held hers up by the stem. "A toast. To Sunshine Creamery. And to second chances."

Her sister wiggled her eyebrows, and for a moment, Lila wasn't sure whether she was referring to the ice cream parlor or the man who had the power to help her save it.

*

Maybe it was the glass of wine, maybe it was the talk with Mary, or maybe it was the realization that nearly a week had passed and the only progress she had made with Sam was nearly falling for him again—*nearly* being the operative word—that made Lila set down her glass, stand up and smooth her skirt, and announce she was going out.

"Out? Where?" Mary's eyes flashed with interest.

"Unfinished business," Lila summarized as she went back into the kitchen.

She was out the door and in a cab five minutes later, her heart thumping all the way down Lake Shore Drive. Only when they finally stopped in front of the upscale hotel Sam was calling home these days, did Lila hesitate. Her nerves fluttered all the way to the front desk, where she casually asked to be connected to his room, hating the way that came out, and wondering if Sam would have the same interpretation. If he'd take it the wrong way. If he'd try to kiss her again.

She sucked in her lower lip.

Resisting him once had been difficult enough, but twice?

The man set down the phone. "I'm afraid he's not in his room. You could try the lobby or the bar."

Lila turned on her heel. She would do just that.

There was no sign of him in the lobby, or in the bar, with its stunning view and cozy seating. Frustrated, Lila stalked back to the elevator, her finger poised over the button that would take her down to the street level, when something caught her eye.

Deciding to give this night one last try, she pressed the button for the pool and sun deck and held her breath. The elevator doors slid open once more and there, doing laps, was Sam.

Lila walked to the edge of the pool, watching as Sam's strong, hard back cut effortlessly through the water. It had been many years since she'd seen his bare chest, and her body warmed at the sight of it, remembering how it felt to run her fingers over his skin, to dig her nails into his back when he pushed into her, his mouth on her neck, his breath in her hair.

She waited patiently as he swam the length of the pool twice more, wondering if he had noticed her yet, but suspecting he hadn't. When Sam set his mind to something, very little could deter him. He was a driven man by nature, and right now his focus was on something other than work. Or her.

Finally, he reached the far end and stood. The surface of the water met him at the hip, revealing a smooth bare torso chiseled with corded muscles. His back to her, he used his arms to lift his body onto the ceramic tile. His navy swim trunks clung to his wet skin, and Lila had to look away.

"Hey!" he called out, his face breaking out in a surprised grin. He walked toward her, water dripping generously from the knees of his shorts and onto the floor. She flitted her gaze down to his waistband, following the trace of hair that began at his belly button.

She took a step back as he neared her.

"What are you doing here?" His brow flinched in curiosity, but there was a telling spark in his eyes.

Lila paused to consider her own reasoning. She hadn't thought this far ahead. She wasn't prone to impulse; if anything, she lived her life in a regimented, structured routine. Only one person had the power to make her forget all rational senses and act on sheer whim, and that person was standing half naked before her.

Damn him.

"So," Sam continued, wandering out onto the sun deck. His damp hair curled slightly over his forehead and he combed it back with his fingers before picking up a towel. "To what do I owe this honor?"

He scanned her face for an explanation, and Lila once again found herself at a complete disadvantage. Her grand plan had made so much sense twenty minutes ago, but now she struggled, feeling foolish. She wasn't here to smooth things over, much less make things easy. If nothing else, she was here to demand an answer. How dare he almost kiss her and then not even bother mentioning it again? And what right did he think he had to waste an entire day that could have been spent working?

"So this is how you've been spending your afternoon, while I've been busy slaving away coming up with ideas for the Reed campaign."

"I had some business matters back at the office to take care of," Sam explained as his jaw hardened. His eyes blazed through hers with indignation. "And I always try to get in at least an hour of exercise. Takes the edge off. Helps me think."

"You ran off in such a hurry . . ." Lila tipped her head and stood tall in her heeled sandals, meeting Sam squarely in the eye. Navy flecks surrounded his large black pupils. She had forgotten about those.

Just one more thing she'd have to work on forgetting.

"Didn't know you were my gatekeeper." He grinned affably and pulled the towel down over his chest.

Lila allowed her gaze to follow the white terrycloth as it circled his sculpted abdomen. She released a measured breath before returning her eyes to his. "You seemed so eager to get to work on the project first thing this morning; I couldn't help wondering if some emergency occurred that would pull you away so quickly."

A smile crept across Sam's face. "You were concerned about me?"

"I didn't say *concerned*." She folded her arms across her chest and met his level stare.

"Aw, Lila . . . you still care," he chided, his grin widening in boyish pleasure. "I knew you did."

Of course I care, Sam, she thought miserably. *That's just the problem.*

"A phone call would have been nice," she said, struggling to make eye contact when he was standing there like that, rubbing a towel all over the very same parts of his body she had once touched.

"I was distracted, Lila. I apologize. Now, can we move on?"

She shifted the weight on her feet. "It's not that simple, Sam. You can't just do something wrong, and then brush it under the rug."

Sam tossed the towel down and nailed her with a look. "Are we talking about today or are we talking about what happened six years ago?"

Lila suddenly felt tired. "I don't want to get in to this again."

"Good," Sam said. "Me either."

He grabbed a white T-shirt from the lounge chair and slipped it over his head, pulling it down over the ridges of his torso. A wave of disappointment fell over Lila that she might never see that bare chest again, and she suddenly felt an overwhelming urge to reach out and touch him.

Luckily, she stopped herself just in time.

Sam tipped his head toward the elevator bank. "Since you're here, why don't we grab dinner?"

Lila's heart skipped a beat when she remembered the reason she was here. Not to stare at her ex-boyfriend's perfectly toned abs, but to fight for something she believed in.

"Actually, I have another idea," Lila said. "A better idea, I should say."

"Oh? Well, I'm all yours," Sam's lips curved slowly, and against her better judgment, Lila couldn't help liking the sound of that.

Chapter Nine

"Where are you taking me?" Sam asked as they climbed out of the cab. He reached into his pocket and took out his wallet, holding up a hand when Lila began to protest.

"To one of my favorite spots in town," Lila said. She needed to clear her head, needed to remind herself of why she was doing this. It wasn't about unrequited feelings or attraction. It was about her family, and preserving their history.

Sam fell in to step beside her. "Should I have worn something a little dressier?"

Lila couldn't help but grin as she glanced at him sidelong, taking in the concerned wrinkle of his brow, the uncertain frown on the mouth that she could still taste if she closed her eyes. "You're fine," she said, glancing at the T-shirt that clung to his broad chest.

She turned away just as quickly and kept her eyes forward. Shop owners were starting to close up now, and most of the storefronts on this stretch were dark. Condensation from air-conditioning units above dripped onto the sidewalk. Lila smiled at a woman watering marigolds in her flower box. She hadn't been back to this part of town in too long—not since they'd cleared out their grandparents' apartment and closed the door one last time on the place they'd called home for the majority of their lives.

Up ahead, at the corner, was Sunshine Creamery. Just the sight of it made Lila's heart swell a little. So many happy times had been spent sitting on a swivel chair at the counter, licking whipped cream off her fingers, and giggling at her grandfather's jokes.

"Here we go," she said, making sure not to slow her pace as she fished out her keys and turned the lock. She pushed through the glass door and flicked on the light, even though the sun was still filtering through the big windows at the front of the room. "Sunshine Creamery. *My* family's business."

"You said your grandparents owned a store. I never knew it was an ice cream parlor." Sam swept his hand over the old soda fountain and let out a low whistle. "Look at this thing!"

"I guess we never talked much about our histories," Lila said. It was easier that way. From an early age she'd learned to put one foot in front of the other, to focus on the present. It was the only way to move forward. The only way to keep on living.

Lila eyed Sam across the room. No good ever came from lingering on the past.

Just to the side of the cash register was a framed photo of Lila with Mary and their grandfather. She must have only been about five at the time, making Mary about three. It wasn't long after they'd come to live with their grandparents. This place was the only thing that cheered them up then—that and the extra sprinkles Gramps added to their sundaes. "Ice cream Sunday," he'd say every Sunday morning, and oh, how they laughed and laughed.

"Ice cream Sunday," Lila whispered. She noticed Sam looking at her, and shook her head, feeling embarrassed. "Sorry, it's something my grandfather used to say. I hadn't thought of it in a long time."

Sam's smile was warm. "This place is amazing, Lila."

Lila looked around the room, trying to see it through his eyes. It was clean but old, with peeling linoleum floors and cracks in the corners of the yellow painted walls. Ghosts of another time seemed to be everywhere: the silent jukebox that had once filled the space with music, the neatly stacked scalloped bowls that once held banana splits. Sunshine Creamery had witnessed more of Lila's history than she would ever know. It had known her as a child, known her mother as a child, her grandmother as a young wife. Her grandfather as a small boy.

She blinked back tears and hugged her arms around

her waist. There was a framed print of a dog licking a fallen cone near the back wall. She focused on it. She'd always loved that picture.

"Why did it close?" Sam asked, dropping onto one of the counter stools. He swiveled to face her.

Lila shifted the weight on her feet, hoping her voice wouldn't betray her emotions. "My grandfather died a few months ago." Damn. No such luck. Her voice was shaky and now her lip was trembling. She cleared her throat, trying to pull herself together.

She needed Sam to see how special this place was. She didn't need to derail the effort by falling apart.

"And you didn't want to take it over?"

Lila laughed softly. "I love this place, but no. I love what I do for work. My sister—" she stopped herself before she said too much. "My sister hopes to carry it on."

Sam jutted his lower lip and nodded as he looked around the room once more. "Good. I'd hate to see an old institution like this disappear."

"Me too." Her voice felt thick. "Mary's been making some ice cream on her time off," she said, brightening. "If you're hungry, I might recommend a scoop of the mint chocolate chip. It's my personal favorite."

"Mint chocolate chip it is, then." He turned in his chair as she came around the counter.

Lila regarded him suspiciously. "Well, that's a first."

"What is?"

Lila opened the freezer, and her heart dropped when she saw the familiar white containers marked with her grandfather's handwriting. They'd been sitting there for months, but Mary still hadn't thrown them out. Lila was grateful for it.

"Oh, I don't know," she said, reaching for one of the newer containers labeled with Mary's loopy cursive. "It isn't often you take a suggestion from me, that's all."

"I'll have you know that I am more than happy to hear your suggestions, Lila. And if they're good ones, I'll agree with them."

Silence fell and Sam's gaze bored through hers. He rubbed at his jaw, heaving a sigh, and Lila drifted her eyes to his mouth, recalling the way his lips felt against hers.

Good grief. If she kept this up, the ice cream was going to melt all over her hands!

She found Gramps's metal scoop next to a pile of notes and paint swatches Mary must have left on her last visit, and reached for a bowl. She'd brought Sam here for a reason. To show him where she came from. To make him understand the importance of tradition.

No better time than the present, she thought with a tightening in her stomach.

"Here you go, sir." Her smile was thin as she tucked a spoon into the ice cream and slid the bowl across the counter.

He took a bite, managing a rueful smile. "It's delicious."

"A family recipe," Lila explained. "Mary's been

practicing them for when she takes over." *If* she takes over, was more like it. There was only so long they could go on carrying the cost of this empty place.

Sam looked at her quizzically. "You're not having any?"

Lila shook her head. "I have an idea I'd like to go over with you." She was proud of what she had come up with, but she had no idea how Sam would react.

Or what would happen if he shot it down.

"When you think of ice cream, what do you feel?" she asked. Sam gave her a long look, but she just said, "Work with me on this."

"Summer. Sweet. Cold. Creamy. Childhood. Carefree." A shadow crossed his face.

Lila's pulse began to race. "I think of holidays, weekends, staying up past my bedtime, sitting on a park bench, licking a cone, my hands getting sticky. I think of peace, quiet. The sun on my face. Sitting in silence, enjoying the simplicity of the moment. Happiness." She swallowed the lump that had formed in her throat. "I think of this place."

She said nothing more as she walked to the back room, grabbed the industrial-sized bag of sugar, and somewhat awkwardly carried it back into the main room. Depositing it on the counter with a loud *thud*, she pointed to the label.

"Reed Sugar." She watched Sam for a reaction. He was careful not to offer one. "None of this would have been possible without Reed Sugar."

Sam slid his empty bowl to the side and blew out a sigh as he set his elbows on the counter. "Okay, I'm listening."

"An ice cream parlor is . . . a cheerful place. A celebratory place. A special place. It's innocent. It's tradition. It's timeless. You come here after a bad day to cheer up. Memories are made here. Happy ones. Ones you want to share with your kids. Ones you want to hold on to, ones that make you just feel good. Reed Sugar can make all that possible. Reed Sugar . . . the sweeter side of life."

Sam nodded thoughtfully, saying nothing, his gaze never straying from hers. Lila held her breath, waiting for his response, bracing herself for a snide remark.

He rubbed a hand over his mouth and chuckled. "I think you may be on to something."

"Really?" Lila gasped.

Sam's gaze traveled over her face. "I'm impressed, Lila. It's not what I usually go for, but . . . I like it. I like it a lot."

She regarded him suspiciously, waiting for a hint of a smirk, but none appeared. "Well, good. Excellent. I'm glad we're moving forward." *Just stay professional, Lila. Don't let him see how much this means to you. How badly you need it.*

She came around the counter and slid onto the stool next to his. "My grandfather's up there smiling." She grinned at Sam, but his smile slipped.

"I'm sure he's proud of you." There was an edge to his tone, a sadness to his eyes. "You know, as much as I wish we could change the past, part of me feels like you ended up exactly where you were meant to be."

"You mean the ice cream parlor?" Lila laughed softly.

"I mean, here, near your family, doing your own thing. Doing it well. You always believed in your ideas, even if I didn't. Now you're free to pursue them. Not everyone is so lucky."

"Says the man who is revered—"

Sam was shaking his head. "Says the man who is still waiting to make someone proud."

Lila searched his face for a hint of the ego, the big personality, the swagger. But the man sitting next to her seemed lost and sobered. "You look tired," she said quietly.

He nodded. "I am tired. Tired of letting people down. I let you down."

"Sam . . ." She shook her head.

"You know you're still the prettiest damn girl I ever kissed." Sam grinned, and Lila pushed back the emotions that were firing to the surface.

Before she could react, Sam leaned in and skimmed her lips with his. The kiss was light and slow, causing a current of desire to dash down Lila's spine and a wave of hunger to throb deep within her. She'd missed this. The feel of his mouth on hers, the warmth of his body. The touch of his hand.

Slowly, she opened her mouth to his, letting him in. He kissed her slowly, then, coming off the stool to pull her closer, with more need. She sighed into his mouth, as their lips explored each other and her insides pooled with warmth. His hands were on her back, and then lower, on her hips. She set a hand tentatively on his chest, feeling the beat of his heart under her palm, and wrapped the other around his back, holding him tight.

Breaking the kiss, he pulled away, his eyes tearing through hers, dark with unspoken emotion.

Lila brushed her hair off her face and brought a finger to her lips. "You know, I think I might have some of that ice cream after all," she said, edging backward, toward the counter.

Sam stood where he was, watching her but saying nothing. She took a bowl from the stack and lifted the scoop. She had forgotten to put away the ice cream and it was already soft.

"Seconds?" she asked Sam, lifting a brow.

He nodded. "Seconds would be great," he said, and Lila bit her lip to hide her smile as she dug into the ice cream.

If she didn't know better she might just think he was referring to something other than dessert.

*

Sam's mind was still on Lila as he stepped out of the cab and breathed in the chilly night air. The hotel glowed in the night, casting a warm light over Michigan Avenue and the high-end retailers that were now closed for the day. He knew this should be his reality check—a reminder of how far he had come—but as he stood outside the grand entrance, alone with the stiffly uniformed staff, he felt as conspicuous as if he were standing in a spotlight. Exposed for what he was. He could almost see his grandmother looking down on him, shaking her head in disappointment.

The hotel lobby was empty and quiet. Sam wandered toward the elevator bank, his tread silent despite the heaviness in each step. He pressed the button and stuffed his hands into his pockets, rolling back on his heels as he waited for the doors to open.

It was late, and he hadn't been sleeping well lately, but he needed something to take the edge off, to rid his mind of everything that was clouding his judgment and leaving him restless. If he went to bed right now, he would do nothing but lie there and stare at the ceiling. He stepped off the elevator and walked straight to the bar.

"Scotch," he told the bartender, as he settled onto a stool. He studied the television, noting the baseball scores, and then accepted the glass tumbler with a nod. He swirled the ice and took a sip, waiting for it to take its desired effect.

Lila thought he couldn't understand where she came from, what mattered most. It had taken everything in him not to tell her just how wrong she was—how alike they were. That he knew what it was like to come home to a cramped apartment, but to not care. That he did value family over money, contrary to popular belief.

He took another sip. His stomach burned—not from the drink but from the decision he'd made all those years ago. He'd told himself it was about finding out where he came from, but sometimes, when he thought back on his childhood, happy and simple as it was, he wondered if all he'd really done was turn his back on the person he really was, and the man he was meant to be.

He supposed he should be relieved that the pitch was coming along. That he would most likely secure the account. That the agency would maintain its reputation. That his father might be proud. That his brother might stop reminding him of his place in the family.

But all he could think of was that creaky old rocking chair his grandmother used to sit in when she read him stories, and the picture of her he kept in his apartment, serving as his only reminder of her.

He wished he could have told Lila about her tonight. Hell, he'd wished he could tell Lila about her many times. She would have understood in a way that other girls wouldn't have cared to—they wanted to see Sam Crawford, son of Preston, with all his money and flash. But Lila . . . She didn't really like that side of him, did she?

He took another swig of his drink, hoping to numb the memory of her, to curb the excitement he felt at seeing her again tonight. It was no use. She had wormed her way into his mind, and nothing he tried made him capable of banishing her. She was an itch that needed a scratch—he couldn't escape her or the memory of her smooth skin under his. He was never one to get attached to a woman like this before; normally it was easy for him to walk away, to enjoy a night together and move on. But with Lila . . . one kiss was all he needed to leave him wanting more.

An uneasy feeling began a slow creep. Something told Sam he had met his match. And he wasn't quite sure what to do about it.

Chapter Ten

Sam slid his key card into its slot, waited for the beep, and let himself into the quiet hotel suite. He'd thought a run along the lakeshore path would help him clear his head, but there was no escaping the noise that jumbled his thoughts and clouded his judgment. He grabbed a bottle of water from the mini-fridge and checked his phone. No missed calls. He scanned his inbox, skimming a few e-mails and making a mental note to come back to several others once he had powered up his laptop.

From the phone at the wet bar, Sam called the front desk and placed an order for lunch. Stripping his sweaty clothes from his body, he turned the shower to the hottest setting, until steam fogged the mirror. His muscles ached, and a chill had settled into his skin from the air-conditioning. He contemplated scheduling a massage at the hotel's spa, but decided against it. He'd already taken a long enough break for the day. It was time to get down to business.

He turned off the taps, toweled off, and dressed quickly. Padding barefoot into the living room, he called the office. Rex answered on the second ring.

"Any new developments I should be briefed on?" Sam inquired.

"I just can't reiterate enough how much we need this Reed account, Sam." Rex's voice was gravelly, but there was a hint of a threat in his tone that couldn't be overlooked.

Sam felt his temper stir. He'd been working for PC Advertising since he graduated from college—only two years after Rex—but somehow his brother considered himself the mentor, the lead. Sam knew deep down that Rex still felt the need to cement his role as the legitimate child of Preston Crawford just as much as Sam intended to carve out a place for himself. No matter how far the brothers had come in their relationship, insecurities ran deep for both of them.

"I heard you the first time, Rex," he said evenly. "I was actually referring to Dad."

"He's been his same grouchy self," Rex replied, and for once, that was a cause for relief. "Obviously there's no telling what kind of setback he'd have if he knew what was going down at the agency. I'm hoping it doesn't come to that."

Sam set his jaw. "I told you not to worry about things with Reed. I'm on it."

"Well, you'd better be. If you don't pull this off, we're going to lose our standing."

"I think you're being fatalistic," Sam said mildly. There was a knock on the door, and Sam put his brother on hold to answer it. The room service cart was wheeled in and Sam tipped the service person, even though his appetite was suddenly lost and the smell was making his stomach churn. He waited until the door had closed before picking up the phone again, anger coursing in his veins at the pressure his brother was placing on him. "What are the account managers doing, Rex? There are hundreds of companies of the same caliber as Reed Sugar and Jolt Coffee."

"Of course there are, but that's not the problem. The problem is time, Sam. You have a little more than a week to pull this thing off. No one wants to go down with a sinking ship. People choose us because we're the best. Because all the other big players are with us. If that goes away . . . Everything is riding on this, so don't screw it up."

A week. Sam rubbed the back of his neck, frowning at the tension in his upper back. Endless problems could arise between now and then, but only one thing was certain.

"I have no intention of screwing this up," he told his brother.

No intention at all.

*

Penny had already left for the day by the time Lila closed her laptop. She leaned back in her chair and stretched her arms wide. It had been a productive day, and a quiet one, too. No word from Sam, not that this bothered her. Too much.

She inhaled sharply when she thought of that kiss. The way his lips had felt on hers, the heat of his hands on her skin. The racing of his heart under his T-shirt. The hard wall of his chest pressed close to her body.

She shook away the image. They'd slipped. Fallen back on old habits. It was a mistake. And it wouldn't happen again. It *couldn't* happen again.

Soon, Sam would go back to New York, and she'd . . . Well, she and her sister would be able to reopen Sunshine Creamery. She'd come to her office every day, listen to Penny's stories about her latest disastrous Internet date (the last one had slid her the bill when the meal was over), and watch the little bluebird pop out of the cuckoo clock. She'd get her coffee from Hailey, wave to Jim Watson, and sit on her fire escape with Mary. And soon, Sam would be a thing of the past again.

Lila wandered into the small waiting area. "Good night, Fred," she said, as she flicked the lights and closed the door behind her.

"Talking to your plants now?" a deep voice behind her said.

Lila jumped and flung her hand to her chest. She could hear its steady drum as she looked down through the propped open door of the vestibule to see Sam standing at the base of the stairs, giving her a lopsided grin. "You surprised me. What . . . what are you doing here?"

Sam held up two large take-out bags. "Hungry?"

Lila hesitated with her hand on the iron rail. She hadn't eaten anything since a croissant at the café at eleven, but her appetite vanished when she locked on those blue eyes.

She never should have allowed herself to kiss him. Now . . . now it was all she could think about.

Sam's grin was boyish as she met him on the sidewalk. "I remember you liked sushi." His voice was deep and smooth, and it sent her mind into a tailspin of memories and conflicted desires, bringing her back to those days and nights in New York, each one perfectly tainted with an image of Sam.

"Every Friday night." Her heart tugged a little when she thought of their ritual, and the way she looked forward to it each week. It was special, she thought, that they had a tradition of their own. She'd dared to hope it would be the first of many.

She hadn't eaten sushi since she'd left New York, even though it had once been her favorite food. Dramatic, yes, but more than anything, indicative. She'd never gotten over him. Six years and terrible behavior had done nothing to erase all the good times she still clung to. And now . . . She glanced at him sidelong, hating the way it felt so nice to fall into step beside him, to walk with him through her neighborhood, to enjoy that little tingle that zipped down her spine every time he smiled at her. Now she was starting to wonder if she'd ever get over him again.

They walked to Lincoln Park and settled on the cool grass in a little corner that was always empty and shielded by colorful flowering shrubs in bright shades of purple and pink. Sam took the boxes of sushi out of the bags and handed her a set of wooden chopsticks.

"I have a little something else, too." From the second bag he pulled out a bottle of champagne and two paper cups. "The best I could do," he said, grinning. He took an army knife from his pocket, flipped up the corkscrew, and handed it to her, his skin brushing hers at the exchange. Lila's fingers stilled, heated by the touch, but a shiver ripped down her spine.

Ridiculous! It was probably just the wind.

Lila pushed the tip of the corkscrew into the cork as Sam began plating the sushi. Every so often he stopped to check on her progress, and she could make out a hint of amusement in his expression as he leaned over her shoulder. He was so close, so warm and near, she could have sworn she felt his breath on her neck.

She focused on releasing the cork, trying to ignore the way his leg was now skimming hers, creating a tingle that made her body harden. She had to keep her heart out of this. So what if she was attracted to Sam? Surely lots of women were. It didn't mean anything could ever come from it . . . nothing good anyway.

She glanced sidelong to see a shadow of amusement pass over his face. "Need help?" he asked, and Lila hesitated, forgetting for a moment what he was asking of her until he leaned over and wrapped his hand around hers, fumbling with the device. The trace of his fingers on her own sent an electric current rolling through her and she quickly pulled her hand back. She couldn't fight the way his heat made her body respond and her mind race.

The cork popped, causing them both to jump a little. Lila laughed, happy to release her nerves, until she realized she'd fallen right back against his arm.

God help her. His chest rose and fell with each breath, and she sunk against him, enjoying the subtle motion.

Sam's voice was thick and low in her ear. "So, maybe we should talk about what happened last night."

Lila stiffened and leaned forward. If he was here to let her down gently, he had another thing coming. She would never give him that satisfaction. Not the second time around.

"I'm a big girl and I took it for what it was." There. The words were spoken with less emotion than she felt. Sure, a part of her had wanted that kiss to mean something—to promise her a future that could make up for the past—but she was smart enough to know better. Sam couldn't offer her that, as much as she wished that he could.

"And what was it?" Sam asked, lifting a brow.

"An indiscretion," Lila said, inching herself away from him.

Sam's eyes locked with hers. He nodded and finally said, "Well, I can't stop thinking about it."

Lila's heart soared and she quickly pushed it back in place, where it belonged. He was in town for another week. That was it. Their past was rotten and they had no hope for a future. All they had was the present. Right now.

He reached out and traced his finger down the slope of her neck and Lila's skin prickled with pleasure. She grinded her teeth. It couldn't be this easy. Not now, after everything.

"Is that the reason you were so quick to agree with my idea for the campaign?" She had to ask. She had to be sure.

Sam knitted his brow. "Lila. Have you ever known me to sugarcoat anything when it comes to business?"

Lila sighed. "I don't see a point in this, Sam. You live in New York, I live here."

"I think you're just determined to argue with me."

Lila arched a brow. "Argue with you? I'm just stating a fact."

Sam offered a casual grin, his confidence unwavering. "I have a feeling that I can persuade you—"

"Persuade me? Sam, this isn't an advertising campaign. I know where I stand on this issue, and I'm not going to change my mind." Or at least, she was trying not to. She squirmed under his penetrating gaze, wishing she hadn't said a word. That he couldn't prove her wrong.

Finally, he pulled back. Poured the champagne and handed her a cup.

"What's the occasion?" Lila asked.

"To Reed Sugar. And . . . to unexpected surprises."

Lila took a small sip and set the cup down, struggling to balance it on the grass. She needed to keep a cool head tonight. "Are you that shocked that I came up with an idea you actually like?"she asked, managing a wry grin.

Sam gave her a long look. "I was referring to you and me, Lila. To finding each other after all this time."

Oh. Lila swallowed hard and shifted on the grass as best she could in her skirt. She reached for the champagne. One more sip. She needed it.

Okay, maybe two more sips.

Sam tore into a pocket of soy sauce and stirred in some wasabi. Lila helped herself to a California roll, happy for the distraction. They ate without talking, the way only two people who knew each other could without feeling the strain of silence, the weight of having to think of something to say. Only this was one time where Lila suspected Sam had a lot to say, and contrary to her better judgment, she was desperate to hear it.

"I apologize for the lack of dessert," Sam said when they'd polished off the four rolls. "But nothing could really top that ice cream I had last night."

"Ice cream is always a little sweeter in the summer," Lila agreed with a smile. She knew Mary would love to reopen Sunshine Creamery before the end of the season. With any luck, she just might be able to. "But then, most things are."

"Even me?" Sam cocked an eyebrow, and his mischievous grin made her laugh.

"Yes," she admitted. "Even you."

*

Sam leaned back against the grass, resisting the urge to reach up and pull Lila back with him, to roll on top of her, bury his mouth in the crook of her neck, and kiss her until she moaned. She was right. Last night had been a mistake—an indiscretion. Past or no past, they lived in different worlds. They always had.

His jaw tensed. *Not always.*

"You really light up when you talk about your grandparents," he said, smiling sadly, thinking of the woman who had raised him, the way he couldn't think of her without his gut burning with shame.

Lila shrugged and glanced down at him over her shoulder. Her hair spilled over her back, catching the last golden rays of the sunset. "They were really special. They didn't have much, but we never even noticed. We were happy, which is about all we could have hoped for after our parents . . ."

Sam smiled sadly. "You're lucky to have had them," he said.

Catching the edge in his tone, Lila looked at him

sharply. "Is everything okay?"

Sam propped himself up on an elbow. "There's a lot going on back in New York right now. I'm a bit . . . tense."

"Work or family?"

"My father—" Sam stopped himself. He pushed himself up to a sitting position and frowned at the grass. "My father and I have never been close," he said, unable to hold back what was so forefront on his mind.

Lila tilted her head. "Was it always that way, even growing up?"

This was it. This was the moment he could tell her the truth—the dark past he'd kept hidden from everyone in his new life. The shameful family secret that no one could ever speak about, that would taint the Crawford legacy.

Sam cleared his throat. "I didn't grow up with my father," he said.

A little wrinkle appeared on Lila's forehead. "But . . . I thought your parents were married."

"My dad is married, yes. But not to my mother."

He stole another glance at Lila, who was doing a damn poor job of disguising her shock. "I'm sorry," she stammered. "I—"

Sam held up a hand. "It's okay. No one knows. Well, a few perhaps, but they know not to say anything." He drew a sharp breath, slicing through the pain in his chest when he thought of his father's choices. "My father had an affair when Rex was just a toddler. And I was the result." He shrugged, but the crease in Lila's face showed that she didn't believe his dismissive attitude anymore than he did. "My mother told him she was pregnant, and he tried to pay her off," Sam said, his voice coarse with sudden emotion. He wasn't used to talking about his family this way. They were who they were, and he saw little point in harping on the facts. But voicing it aloud was cathartic. Even if it did conjure up painful feelings he did his best to stow away. "Guess he didn't need me complicating his life."

Lila shook her head, frowning. "She told you that?"

"No." He ground his teeth, wishing he could stop talking about this, stop thinking about it. That he could block out the painful memories as he'd done for so many years, but the anger inside him needed to be released. "I never knew my mother. She died right after I was born. There were . . . complications."

Silently, Lila reached over and took his hand in hers. He squeezed it tight, without any intention of letting it fall.

Sam huffed out a breath. Shame tightened his chest when he thought of the woman he had never known and only learned about through stories. The woman his father had turned his back on. "I grew up with my grandmother, actually. My mother's mother."

Lila blinked. "Just like me," she said so softly he could barely hear her words.

Sam brushed his thumb over her fingers. They felt so small and soft in his. "Just like you."

"So how did you find your father?" Lila asked.

"My grandmother died when I was a freshman in college, and I found my birth certificate when I was cleaning out her apartment."

Lila's frown deepened. "Apartment?"

"Yeah, I grew up in Queens. Not exactly Park Avenue, like you were expecting." He arched a brow.

Lila paused. "No," she eventually said, shaking her head. "Not what I thought at all."

"Life was tough at times. We struggled." And he was still struggling. Struggling to be the best and stay at the top. Only not for money. Not like people thought.

"But the money your father—"

Sam shook his head. "My mother didn't accept it. She was too proud."

"Surely your grandmother could have reached out to him . . ."

Sam rubbed the back of his neck and stared out at the park, recalling the hardened look that would pass over his grandmother's face whenever Sam asked about his father. "No. No, I don't think she wanted anything to do with Preston Crawford, even if it might have made her life a little easier." He looked back at Lila. "It's the reason I waited until she died to really start looking for him. I could sense that he was out there somewhere, but I didn't press it. I knew that she thought I was better off without him."

And more and more, he was beginning to wonder if she was right. He loved his father, but he couldn't be sure the feeling was reciprocated. And now . . . He thought of the ticking clock, the memories that were fading every day. Now maybe it never would.

Lila's soft hazel eyes were wide. "I had no idea. You never said anything."

"I can't always say that I'm proud, but it's something I needed to do. I had no family left after my grandmother died. At first, it was about fulfilling a childhood curiosity, of just meeting him. Then . . ." He gave a sad smile. "Well, then it became something more."

Lila lifted her eyebrows and inhaled a deep breath, but said nothing. She clearly didn't agree with his father's choices any more than he did. "And Rex?" she eventually asked.

"Oh, Rex will always be the real son. Guess I should just be happy I got a brother out of this deal, even if he can be difficult."

"You want your father's love," Lila observed, and Sam had to square his jaw to hold back the building emotions.

"I've done everything I could to earn his approval, to prove to him I'm no different than Rex. I changed my name, taking his, trying to make him see that I am every bit his own. Maybe someday he'll actually believe it."

Or maybe, he thought, falling back on that old fear, *maybe all these sacrifices were for nothing.*

Her hand was still on his, warm and steady. He grazed his thumb over her fingers again, catching her eye. Her lips parted slightly, and he waited for her to pull back, to distance herself from him, but she didn't.

Sam reached over and tucked a strand of Lila's hair behind the slender curve of her ear before leaning in and whispering, "I'm going to kiss you again right now, Lila. And this time, we're not going to call it a mistake."

He ran his mouth down to her lobe and took it gently in his teeth. Lila sighed, and he felt her smile against his cheek. He slid one arm around her waist as his lips trailed softly to hers, and he kissed her softly at first, slowly, wanting to savor her sweet taste. Her body rose and fell in beat with his own, and he pulled her closer, feeling the swell of her breasts against his chest, laying her back against the cool grass. Her hair spilled around her as she smiled up at him, and he brushed a tendril from her forehead, before leaning to kiss her once more, and hopefully not for the last time.

*

Her lips still tingled from his kiss. Her heart still pounded in her chest. She took another step. They'd reached the second-floor landing. The building felt quiet and still, with only the faint sound of a television coming from the first-floor unit. Sam was in her building, in her home, in her safe place. The little corner of the world she had carved out for herself after he had ruined her life.

The door to her apartment flung open before she could try the knob.

"Well there you are!" Mary exclaimed. "I've been waiting for you for over an hour. I finally gave up and—

Oh." She stopped at the sight of Sam. Her eyes drifted slowly back to Lila. "Oh, I *see*! Well, don't let me *interrupt* anything. I was just leaving you a note. I got an extra shift tonight. So . . ." She blinked rapidly at Sam.

"Mary, I'd like you meet Sam Crawford. Sam, this is my sister."

"Hello." Sam extended a hand, and Mary beamed as she took it.

"I've heard so much about you, Sam," she stage whispered.

"All good, I hope?" Sam winked.

"Well . . ." Mary giggled, and Lila tightened her grip on her handbag. Mary was loyal, but she was also entirely too forgiving. But then, unlike Lila, she was yet to really have her heart broken.

Lila hoped she never would.

"See you in the morning then?" Lila felt her cheeks begin to burn. She could only imagine how this looked to Sam. A night alone in her apartment. A bed just a few feet away from the living room sofa. Suddenly, the night held more possibilities than she could have planned for, or maybe even hoped for.

Mary's lips twisted. "Oh, you can bet on it," she said pointedly, as she jogged down the stairs.

Lila sighed as she stepped into her apartment and held open the door to let Sam pass. The dried wreath she had bought one Saturday morning at the market hung on the door. Now Sam would know that wreath. Now Sam would walk into her home as casually as he had strode back into her life, only to slide right out of it a week later.

Or maybe this time it would be different.

"Home sweet home," she said.

"Your sister seemed nice," Sam observed as she closed the door behind him. "I was sort of thinking she'd punch me in the nose or something."

Lila couldn't fight her smile. "Now why would she do that?"

Sam grinned back, and Lila relaxed into the moment. It felt good to be honest like this, to acknowledge the past. It was the only way either of them was going to ever move past it.

Her heart sped up when she considered what this meant. If there was a future between them. Or if this brief time together was just a way of leaving things off on a better note than they had before. A bittersweet good-bye, instead of just a bitter one.

She followed Sam into the living room, where moonlight seeped through the windows, illuminating her most cherished possessions. She had to admit the room looked pretty—almost romantic even—in the natural glow. She hesitated for a moment to turn on a lamp, but then, catching Sam's heated stare, she quickly flicked the switch, her pulse racing.

A photograph of her parents sat on the end table, just below her hand. She was five years old at the time; she could tell by the yellow polka-dot bathing suit she was wearing—she loved that thing. Her mother was wearing a pink sundress, the hand that wasn't tightly wrapped around Lila was shielding her eyes, blocking out the sun that glistened off the lake. Mary sat on their dad's lap, round-faced and smiling. None of them could have known this photo would be the last of its kind. That by the next summer, half the people in this picture would be gone. That one rainy night and a slick back road would change their family forever—that Lila and Mary, tucked into their beds while the babysitter did her homework downstairs, would have no idea their parents were never coming home.

Lila swallowed hard and closed her eyes to the photo.

"Have you lived here long?" Sam was asking, and she was happy for the distraction.

"Since I moved back," she said. *Back from New York.* The implication hung in the room. "We like it here. The neighbors are quiet, and I was lucky to find an office within walking distance."

"This is the same picture that you have at the ice cream parlor." Sam pointed to the photograph he'd seen last night. Mary had set this one in a silver frame on the mantel.

Lila nodded. "It's a special one. That place means a lot to us. It's actually why getting this new account is so important to me. I'm planning on using the money to help Mary reopen the shop. It's expensive, and there's a lot of work to be done on it. She'd run it on her own, but . . . It's our family place. Gramps wanted us both to have it. It was his dying wish, so to speak."

"Then you can't let it go," Sam said.

Lila's heart skipped a beat. "No. I can't. I just hope nothing happens to mess up this account."

Sam nodded thoughtfully. "That makes two of us," he said softly, taking a step closer. He set a hand on her waist and brushed the hair from her cheek with the other. "Tomorrow we'll have to put our heads together and come up with some ideas for the design team. But tonight . . ."

Lila inhaled sharply as his mouth met hers again. Her body was stiff beneath his touch, wanting to resist it as much as she craved it. He kissed her again, lacing his tongue with hers, and she sighed into his mouth.

His breathing turned heavy as he pulled her to him, his hands exploring her waist, gently tugging at her blouse until his fingers tickled her skin. Her body warmed quickly with the heat of his, and she waited with growing need for his lips to move to her mouth. She craned her neck, inhaling the musk of his skin, as his mouth traced patterns on her neck, winding this way and that, until she tightened and tensed, aching for more.

Breaking their kiss, she took his hand and led him into her bedroom. The light from the moon spilled shadows over the walls and duvet cover as he eased her onto the bed. Slowly, Sam began releasing each button of her blouse. He ran a hand over her lace bra and released her breasts, caressing them slowly until he lowered his mouth. Lila arched her back to smother a groan and ran her hands through his hair as he teased her with her teeth.

Finally releasing her, he pushed back long enough to remove his T-shirt and reveal the smooth contours of his hard chest. Lila reached up and grazed the wide span of his chiseled shoulders with her fingertips, allowing her hands to slowly trace down the curve of his biceps to the smooth plank of his chest. His skin was hot and smooth under her touch, and she held her breath as she waited for him to lower himself to her, to feel the strength of his body against hers.

Her skirt was hitched up around her waist, and Sam ran a hand firmly down the length of her thigh as he pushed himself between her legs, then circled his fingers around, under the back of her knee, and up, up, up, until . . . She dug her nails into his back, feeling the weight of his warm body on her chest, as his fingers pulsed and stroked and his lips again found her mouth.

His kiss was hungry and deep and she pushed herself into him, needing him closer. She had loved this man. She had waited and hoped and then tried to forget. But now, she would just enjoy this moment.

Chapter Eleven

Sunlight filtered through the pale blue linen curtains in Lila's bedroom, a breeze through the half-open window causing them to billow at the floor. Birds chirped on the fire escape, feasting off the seeds Mary bought for the feeder.

Lila stirred and then smiled into her pillow when she remembered last night—the hunger in his kiss, the swell of him inside her. She'd never have imagined they could have a moment like that again, and she wanted to savor it, and hold on to it for as long as she could.

She closed her eyes, clinging to the memory of Sam's touch, the feel of his warm skin next to hers, the taste of his lips. Rolling over, she spread her arm out wide, her fingers reaching for the smooth wall of his chest, but all she felt instead were cold cotton sheets on a flat mattress.

She sat upright, breathing a little easier when she saw Sam sitting at her desk chair near the window, tapping on his phone. He gave her a lazy smile when he noticed her, but something in his eyes seemed flat and faraway.

"There you are," she said sleepily, bringing the sheet up a little higher. "How long have you been up?"

"A while." Sam looked tense and he made no movement toward coming back to bed. Instead, he stood, stuffed the phone in his pocket, and set his hands on his hips. "Lila, I'm sorry. I have to go. Something's come up in New York. My brother texted me this morning. It's . . . important."

She held the sheet tighter to her chest, wishing her robe was within arm's reach. "You mean, right now?"

He nodded. "Right now. I booked a flight. The cab is already downstairs waiting to take me back to the hotel to change. It's important," he stressed again.

Lila frowned. Of course it was important. With Sam, business always was. She nodded, trying to hide her disappointment. If she said anything, it wouldn't come out right, and she didn't even know what there was to say. It was a work day, and Sam had to work.

But something in his eyes told her it was more than that, and that's what troubled her.

A sour taste filled her mouth. It was all about his damn career. It always was, and it always would be.

"What about Reed?" she asked, forcing herself to set aside her emotions and focus on the goal they still shared.

"We still need to come up with the presentation."

"We'll deal with it when I get back."

"Which is when?" Their meeting was only a week away and there were still hours of work to be done. They might have the general concept, but coming up with something to really wow a company as big as Reed was another hurdle altogether.

"I don't know." He looked distracted as he pulled on his shoes and tied the laces.

"You don't *know*?" Lila repeated in disbelief.

"I'll brainstorm on the plane," he added. "I'll go over things with the team."

"I'm part of this team," Lila reminded him. "Maybe I should book a ticket."

"*No.*" His tone was forceful, his gaze fiery. Perhaps noticing her shocked expression, he raked a hand through his hair and heaved a sigh. "Look, this shouldn't take long. I'll be back in time for the meeting."

Lila nodded. Back in time for the meeting. It was all business again.

She should have kept it that way.

"Here I thought maybe we'd have breakfast together this morning or something." She hated the hurt that had crept into her voice. She'd promised herself a long time ago that she'd never let this man see her cry, never let him know how badly he had hurt her. Now he'd done it all over again. And she'd let him.

Foolish girl.

"They need me back right away. I'm sorry, Lila. I really

am." The expression in his eyes was pained. He had one hand on her bedroom doorknob, waiting for her to say good-bye.

Knowing she had no other choice and, no real hold on him for that matter, she nodded her head.

His eyes lingered on her for a hopeful second before he drew a long breath and turned. Lila watched with a heavy heart as he disappeared from the bedroom, and then, out the front door. No kiss good-bye. No mention of last night. No hint of a repeat.

A matter of hours ago he had been in her arms, and now she was alone. Even if it was her own damn fault, the knowledge did little to make her feel better. Lila looked miserably around the empty bedroom, all trace of Sam suddenly gone from her home, and allowed the tears to spill freely down her cheeks.

She had thought this time it could be different, but nothing had changed. Not one damn thing.

She was in love with Sam, whether she liked it or not. And right now, she didn't like it one bit.

*

The thirty-mile drive from LaGuardia Airport to Greenwich, Connecticut, felt more like one hundred. Sam glanced impatiently at his watch for the third time in half an hour, and only relaxed once the driver pulled onto the residential road that had become familiar to him in the twelve years since he'd first come here on a cold fall day, his junior year of college.

The stone mansion was set far back from the street, sheltered behind tall iron gates and a crisp boxwood hedge. A circular drive rounded at the end of the manicured lawn, just outside the front door, where oversized urns were filled with topiaries and small red flowers. Even now, the place felt daunting, just as it had on that first, stiff visit. The halls seemed as vast as building lobbies, the grounds as large as the parks he used to play in as a kid. Everything was in its place—not a curtain off its hook, not a magazine discarded on an end table. Vases of fresh flowers were set on coffee tables and changed weekly. Professional photos were displayed in silver frames, alongside porcelain figurines, dusted daily. He knew some might take one look at the house and everything inside it and feel the need to claim it, to take what was theirs, but Sam hadn't been impressed. He'd been furious. And sad. And hopeful.

He still was.

His brother met him at the door, looking grim and tired. His brown hair, so much like Sam's, was unkempt and tousled.

"How is he?" Sam asked, dreading the answer. He followed Rex into the foyer and set his briefcase down on a console table, and then, on second thought, moved it to the floor. Even now, he still worried about breaking something, and the crystal vase holding a dozen yellow roses looked like it could tip at the slightest bump.

"Better than yesterday, but still not great. He's on the

veranda," Rex said, leading the way. "It took him a while to calm down last night. He lashed out at the new housekeeper. She gave me her notice an hour ago."

The irritability was another part of the illness, and the revolving door of staff at the house wasn't helping matters. "He needs a routine," Sam said.

"Don't tell me what my father needs," Rex said icily.

Sam drew a fist at his side, and squeezed it until his hand cramped. No good would come from taking a swing at his brother right now, no matter how badly he wanted to. They were both stressed as hell.

Still, he hated when Rex did this. Claimed his standing, reminded Sam of his place in the family. The hostility had faded over the years, and a part of Sam understood Rex's dilemma. His father had cheated on his mother. Sam admired the side of Rex that stayed true to her, but he didn't appreciate being blamed for their father's indiscretion.

It was obvious that Rex had slept very little, as evidenced by the twelve texts he'd sent Sam over the course of last night—ones that hadn't been received until this morning, when Sam woke up in Lila's sunny bedroom, his arm tight around her waist, his nose buried in her hair. He could have stayed like that all day, but the phone wouldn't stop vibrating, and he knew he couldn't ignore it forever.

He swallowed hard when he thought of the look on Lila's face this morning. The hurt in her eyes. He'd wanted to explain, to tell her why he had to run off like that, but he couldn't. And now . . . He shook his head clear. He couldn't think about Lila right now.

"Tell me again what happened," Sam said, and his brother started at the beginning, giving more detail to the bits and pieces that had come in through the texts. Their father had agreed to meet Rex for dinner. Rex had waited for an hour before texting Sam. After two hours, he'd called the police. They'd found Preston in his car, listening to the radio, somewhere near the state border. When they asked where he was going, he'd said he couldn't remember. When they asked where he lived, he couldn't remember that either.

"He's getting worse," Rex stated flatly.

Sam jutted his chin toward the back of the house. "Let's go see him."

Preston was sitting on a wicker chair, sipping iced tea and reading the paper, when Sam and Rex stepped through the open French doors. The pool glistened behind him, barely used, and more for show than anything else, and Sam spotted Rex's mother over in the tennis courts, practicing her serve with a personal trainer.

In pressed khakis and a golf shirt, his father looked no different than the imposing figure Sam had shaken hands with that first confusing day in this house when he was just twenty years old. He'd wondered how the meeting would go. If his father would hug him. If he'd cry, even. Or if he'd simply turn him away. But all he'd done was look hard and deep into Sam's eyes and then thrust out a hand. Sam had let out a long breath and taken it. It was the first thing his father had ever offered him; he wasn't going to overlook it.

"Heard you've been in Chicago," his father boomed now in that rich, deep voice that had once intimidated the hell out of Sam. He hadn't grown up with a man in the house, and the stories his grandmother had told him echoed in his mind those first few years, until Sam knew he had no choice but to push them back.

"I have some meetings with Reed Sugar," Sam said, lifting the pitcher of iced tea from its tray.

"What's the angle?" his father asked, and Sam had to smile. He was still sharp. Still inquisitive. Still eager to be a part of the action.

Sam poured a glass of tea and took a long sip. "We're still ironing out the details."

"*We?*" Preston frowned.

From across the table, Rex glared at Sam. "It's a big client, Dad. We're all involved."

"Good," Preston said, returning to his paper. "I knew I could count on you boys to keep things running. I went for ten years without a vacation; I suppose I've earned a few days away from the office."

Sam took a chair next to his father, feeling uneasy. "It's nice to have a break now and then."

"Ah, but not for too long. Wouldn't want people slacking off now, would I?"

Rex leaned back against the stone railing and gave Sam

a pointed look.

"I'm a little hungry from my flight," Sam said, rising. He moved toward the French doors to the house. Rex was quick to follow. "I think I'll ask the housekeeper to make us some sandwiches."

"Good, good. And ask your mother to join us, too, will you?" Preston looked straight at Sam.

The two brothers froze. In all these years, Sam's mother had never been mentioned. Not with Rex, not with his mother, and not with Preston. Not even when they were alone. It was as if Sam had appeared at the gate, and the details of where he came from were not to be discussed. Once, he had mentioned something about his grandmother, a fond memory he shared over a Christmas dinner. The table had gone silent for several tense minutes, until Rex's mother tactfully turned the conversation to the discussion of the house lights. It seemed a few had burned out a bit early, and someone would need to get a ladder out to fix the problem.

Sam stared back at his father now, his heart pounding in his chest, until he realized that his father meant his wife—Rex's mother. "Sure," he said, and cleared his throat.

He didn't look at Rex as he walked back into the house, into its cool, impeccably decorated rooms, the floors so polished and his legs so unsteady, he felt he might slip. He tried not to think of her, his mother—of what his father had done to her—but sometimes, when he was staring into the cold blue eyes of the man who had abandoned her and his child and gone on to live a comfortable life without so much as a look back, he wondered how he could even be here at all.

"What the hell is going on?" Sam asked, once Rex firmly closed the study door behind them. With its dark wood paneling and leather furniture, it was their father's favorite room in the house. It was where business was discussed. Where most of Sam's connection to his family was forged.

Now, standing in here, Sam realized just how much he hated this room. It was dark, and heavy, and it was empty. There were no framed photographs. No happy memories. It was cold. Like his father.

Rex walked over to the liquor cabinet and poured himself a drink. "You heard him. He thinks he took a few vacation days. He plans to come into the office next week!"

Sam frowned. "Do you think he really will?"

"Beats me." Rex downed his drink. The only sound that could be heard was from the ticking of the old clock on the bookshelf.

"Can we really stop him?" Sam asked.

"Have we ever really been able to stop him from doing anything once he sets his mind to it?" Rex poured himself another drink and took a thoughtful sip. "If he finds out about Jolt Coffee, he's going to flip. Or try to get them back. And given how he's been lately, I don't see that going down very well."

"Surely he understands that accounts are sometimes lost—"

"No, Sam. No, he doesn't. Preston Crawford didn't lose clients. Preston Crawford was the one who brought Jolt on to begin with."

Sam tossed his hands in the air. "Well, he's going to find out."

"He is," Rex agreed. "But I'd rather him not know until we can balance it out with good news. Now, what do you have for Reed?"

Sam told him about Lila's idea and the spin he hoped to put on it. "There's still a lot to go over."

"Well, we don't have time for that," Rex said tersely. "Move the meeting up to Monday. I'll join you."

Sam hesitated, not liking his brother's tone. "But what about Lila?"

His brother shrugged. "What about her?"

Sam tried to keep the temper out of his voice. He'd seen this kind of thing before. He didn't like where this conversation was going. "Reed wants us to use her. They were rather insistent on it."

Rex gave Sam a pitying look. "I know you're smart, Sam, but I've been living and breathing this business since I was old enough to talk. At the end of the day they want the Crawford name on their account. They want the wow factor. They want a campaign that sells. Period."

"They also want Lila Harris to be involved," Sam reiterated.

"And share the fee? Send a message to our clients that

we're willing to lose money when we're paying experienced staff to do better? Why the hell did you agree to this ludicrous arrangement to begin with?" Rex shook his head and scowled. "Let me guess. It's the girl. You couldn't resist. You always had a sore spot for her, as I recall."

"They know about Jolt Coffee," Sam said.

Rex stood perfectly still. "What do you mean, they know about Jolt Coffee?"

"I have no idea what they know or where they heard it, but they knew something was up. From where I sat, it was use the freelancer of their choosing or walk away."

Rex began to chuckle softly. "This is perfect!" he roared, pounding a fist on the mahogany desk. "They have no leverage. They wanted the best of both. Some local copywriter to make them look true to their roots and drive home that family feeling. They knew we had a major client pulling out and they used it to their advantage. Now, what they don't know is that . . . we don't need them."

"What are you saying, Rex?"

"Call Reed and reschedule that meeting for Monday. We do this on our terms and we make them want us even more than we want them."

"It's a huge risk," Sam said.

"It's the only way," Rex disagreed.

Sam held his brother's gaze for a beat and then marched over to snatch the bottle of whiskey from his hand. He poured himself a drink and downed it in one gulp. If he went along with this, he'd be throwing away any hope of something developing with Lila. For good. He'd prove himself to be the man she had thought he was for all these years. The man she despised.

The man he didn't want to be.

"There's no other way, Sam," Rex stressed, sensing his hesitation. "It's for the business. For the family."

For the family. Sam had never even felt like he was a part of this family, and now he was being asked to sacrifice for it. Again. Just once he'd have liked a pat on the back, some recognition for the effort. Just once he'd like someone in this family to admit that he had a whole life before he came into theirs, and take some interest in it.

They tossed the word *family* around when it was convenient for them, but was he even really part of them, or would he forever be on the fringes? He could take the risk, find out the hard way, or he could float along, and continue waiting.

It all boiled down to this moment. It was his decision to make.

Chapter Twelve

"I still can't believe it." Penny shook her head and pinched her lips a notch tighter. "I just can't believe it. I thought this was it, Lila. I thought this was the one."

Lila managed to catch the time on the cuckoo clock behind the visitor chair in her office. She'd been listening to Penny's woes for the last fifty-five minutes, but she didn't mind. It was a distraction from her own troubles. And, it prevented her from picking up the phone and calling the one person she shouldn't. Yesterday, she'd let slide. But today . . .

She had expected to hear from him today. At least about the pitch.

"He looked nothing like his picture. Nothing!" Penny's large eyes filled with tears, and Lila plucked a tissue from the box she kept on her desk and handed it to her assistant. "I must look ridiculous, crying over a man because he was ten years older and at least fifty pounds heavier than his picture, but that's not even it. I mean, sure, I wasn't expecting the missing tooth, but I'm not shallow. And I'm not picky. I just . . . I thought we had a connection."

Now it was Lila's turn to pinch her lips. Sam had opened up to her more the other night than he had in the six months that they'd dated in New York. She'd gone over his words all day, trying to imagine him as a young boy, living with his grandmother in a small apartment, knowing his father had turned his back on him and his mother but still wanting to seek him out. Her heart ached for that boy, and for the softer, sweeter side of Sam she'd always known was there.

Only now, just like last time, she couldn't help worrying it had been overshadowed by the other side of Sam. The Crawford side.

"Our e-mails were so funny. I can't tell you how much I looked forward to them. Every time the inbox pinged, my heart would too." Penny sniffled. "Then when we met? Silence. Nothing to talk about. I started finding excuses for the waitress to come over, just to break the ice. It was awful. Just *awful*. And now . . . no more e-mails to look forward to. Back to square one."

Lila pulled in a breath and released it slowly. She knew the feeling.

"I wish I'd never even met him!" Penny's eyes suddenly blazed with fury. "I wish I'd just left things alone, kept things as they were. Instead, I had to take it too far and ruin everything!"

"By . . . agreeing to meet him in person?" Lila frowned.

"I loved those e-mails, Lila!" Penny cried. She blew her nose loudly. "Why couldn't that have been enough? Why push your luck, you know?"

Oh, Lila knew all right. Just when she was finally starting to heal from the pain of their past, she had to tempt fate once more. What did she ever expect to come from this? At best, Sam was going to be returning to New York while she stayed in Chicago. At worst . . . She plucked another tissue from the box and began twisting it in her hands. There were plenty of worst-case scenarios when it came to Sam Crawford.

The cuckoo clock chimed, and all at once the little bluebird appeared. This time, Lila didn't even jump, but just watched the machine do its thing until all the little figurines slid back behind their doors, and the clock went quiet again. Penny was still sniffling into her wadded tissue, staring despondently at the floor.

"Well, it's five. I guess I'll go home to my empty apartment. Spend another weekend alone."

"Penny!" Lila gave her a smile of encouragement. "You never know. The next one might be it. Life has a way of surprising us like that."

God, she felt like a hack. Why couldn't she listen to her own advice, feel a shred of the optimism she was spewing?

Because her heart felt like it was twisting, that's why. Because she'd let herself fall. She'd let herself care, let herself share.

And because he'd let her in. *He let me in.* She shook her head. She couldn't think about it anymore today. He hadn't called yesterday, or the day before, and it was time to go home. She might even turn off her cell until Monday morning. She just might.

"Come on. I'll walk out with you." Lila gathered a few files and tucked them into her bag, just in case she needed a distraction this weekend. Work was always a good escape; she was fortunate she loved what she did.

She thought of Mary, toiling away at the doctor's office and later, at the bar, and had to hide her face from Penny to mask her sadness. Her sister deserved to have that, too. A sense of pride and ownership. And she could . . . with Sunshine Creamery.

Lila flicked off the light in her office as the women walked into the waiting area. On Penny's desk sat the plant, just as sad and lonely looking as the two of them. "Here. Why don't you take Fred home for the weekend? I think he could use the company."

Penny lifted one of his drooping leaves. "I suppose I could, too." She eyed Lila thoughtfully. "How's the Reed Sugar campaign coming along? Still canoodling with Sam Crawford? Haven't heard from him in a while . . ." She hoisted the plant into her arms and followed Lila out the door.

"Sam had to fly back to New York for business," Lila replied. She turned the key firmly, until she heard it click. "Besides, anything between us is strictly professional."

Penny raised an eyebrow. That little pinch in her lips had returned. "If you say so."

*

By Saturday morning, with no missed calls reported on her phone, and the meeting with Reed just five days away, Lila began to panic. The problem, however, was that she couldn't unravel in front of her sister. And of all days, Mary had the day free.

"I had another great idea last night," Mary said as she skipped down the stairs of their brownstone. "A customer ordered an apple martini, and I thought . . . why not make cocktail-flavored ice cream?"

Lila adjusted her sunglasses as they began their walk to the park. Her canvas tote was empty and ready for the market, even if her heart wasn't in it at all. "You have a real passion for this, Mary. I can't tell you how happy that makes me." *Or how nervous.*

Mary's smile turned shy. "I know I must seem like the flighty sister . . ."

Lila stopped walking for a moment. "Flighty? What are you talking about?"

Mary gave a bashful shrug and kept her eyes on the sidewalk. "I mean, I dropped out of college my senior year—"

"For good reason," Lila pointed out. She still hated that her sister had been forced to do that, but Lila was working at the time, and well, someone had to pay the rent. "My God, Mary, do you know what kind of sacrifice that was for our family? That's hardly something to be ashamed of."

"Yes, but then I never went back," Mary said. "And look at you. How can I ever compete with that?"

"Compete?" Lila shook her head. Had her sister always felt this way? Sadness pulled at her when she considered the possibility. "Mary, I'm hardly the poster child for success. I got fired from my first job out of college after less than a year. I haven't had a boyfriend since . . ." *Sam.* "And I don't see anyone calling, either." Again she thought of Sam. The bastard.

"Yes, but look at how far you've come! You've been back in Chicago, what . . . a little more than six years now? You took a bad situation and turned it into a good one. You work for yourself. You do what you love. You've made it, Lila."

Lila tried to see her life through her sister's eyes. The office she rented on Armitage Avenue was small, but still, it was her own. And working for herself was certainly better than working for a boss. Oh, sure, she had to report to clients or the agencies that brought her on for project work, but the exchanges were more collaborative. It wasn't the same as the stress she'd felt when she was in New York, trying to push ideas through a group, hoping to be heard. She had experienced a level of freedom and respect in her freelance career that she hadn't in all the time she'd worked for PC Advertising. It had been a risk to go out on her own—to forsake the comfort of benefits and a stable salary—but she'd been too rattled by what had happened to try the corporate world again.

She had Sam to thank for that, she supposed.

They'd reached the park by now, but instead of going straight to the farmers market, Lila pulled her sister over to a bench and motioned for her to sit down. "I've been thinking, and even though we said we'd only hold on to Sunshine Creamery through the end of the summer, I'm thinking we should extend our time period."

Mary looked at her quizzically. "What? No."

Lila gritted her teeth. She hated to deflate her sister's spirit, but Mary had too much faith in her. It was time to face reality. "Mary, there's a very good chance I will not get Reed's business. They're a national brand, and it was a long shot from the start."

"Yes, but you know Jeremy!"

"Loosely," Lila pointed out. "We were classmates almost a dozen years ago. It's a warm lead, not a sure thing."

"But what about Sam? He's a big deal. And if Reed insisted on you as the copywriter—"

Lila tried to mask her frustration. "I'm just saying that we don't know what's going to happen yet, and I for one am tired of pinning all my future plans on the whims of one company." *Or one man.*

"But Lila, we've been over this. Even with my second job and your monthly savings, we're barely scraping by. Between the funeral expenses, and the hospital bills, and the taxes on the parlor . . . It doesn't make sense to keep it if we aren't going to reopen it soon."

Lila frowned. "Maybe we could move to a smaller apartment. One I could afford without your share of the rent. Then you wouldn't have to worry about contributing, and you could quit one of the jobs and use that time at Sunshine."

Mary shook her head sadly. "No, Lila. It wouldn't work. Besides, we both know that place needs a lot of work. And that's an upfront cost."

"It's just . . . I know this means the world to you."

"It does," Mary said softly. "I hate to say this, but Gramps was the only father I ever knew. I . . . I don't really remember Mom and Dad." She brushed away a tear that had started to fall. "I'm just not ready to say good-bye yet. I think that pouring all my energy into Sunshine Creamery these last few months has helped me to not think about the loss. It gave me a sense of hope. It gave me a purpose."

Now it was Lila's turn to brush away a tear. She sniffed hard, happy for the shade of her sunglasses. "I'm not going to take that away from you."

Mary patted her hand and squeezed it tightly. "You never could. Just knowing that you support this, that you're doing all this for me . . . I guess we've both made sacrifices for the family." She smiled sadly.

"Sam left," Lila blurted, unable to hold it in any longer.

Mary frowned. "What do you mean, he left?"

"He went back to New York," Lila said. "Wednesday morning."

Mary gave her a knowing smile. "I *thought* I heard some commotion that morning . . . When I came home your lights were out and the door was closed. It was late, so I assumed you were asleep. Are you going to tell me you weren't sleeping alone?"

Lila rolled her eyes. "That's not the point. The point is that he left, and I haven't heard from him since." Three days had gone by without a word. Three entire days. And the meeting with Reed was fast approaching.

"Have you tried calling him?"

Lila hesitated. She'd reached for the phone several times yesterday at the office, but each time she'd stopped herself, telling herself no good would come from it. Silence spoke volumes, and Sam was sending her a message right now. She just wasn't sure what it was. Or if she even wanted to know. "No, I haven't called."

Mary's eyes widened a notch. "Well, did he say when he'll be back?"

"He promised he'd be back in time for the meeting. But we still have a lot to do first. He did promise though." That uneasy feeling had returned, twisting and turning and leaving her nauseous. Lila pressed a hand to her stomach and released a slow breath.

"And do you think he'll keep to that promise?"

Lila looked her sister square in the eye. "I hope so, Mary. I really, really hope so."

*

Sam glanced down at his phone, his chest tightening when he saw the name displayed on the screen. He let it ring again, but the sound bothered him. It nagged a part of his mind he didn't like to touch anymore. The part that was filled with doubt and shame. With the press of a button, he silenced the device, sending the call directly to voice mail.

He knew what Lila would say, the questions she would ask. He didn't have an answer for her. Not about Reed. Not about them. Not yet, anyway.

He bit back the guilt that was building inside him, mixed with desire and a longing for something he wasn't sure he'd ever have. He'd had too much coffee in the last day and not enough sleep. He felt jittery and agitated, and just thinking of Lila caused his pulse to quicken, and not in a good way. He didn't need the distraction right now anymore than he needed emotion to factor into this.

What he needed was to clear his head. To be honest with himself. To stop living a double life and start living the life he wanted. *Really* wanted.

For years he'd thought it was the Crawford name, the security of being Preston's son. But the perks that came with that were little reward for the cost—for the sacrifices he'd made.

He knew that the Crawfords had their flaws, and he

knew his grandmother had shielded him from ever knowing them for that reason, but something deep inside him could never rest. For twelve years he had lived as one of them, lived this life so different from the one he'd known for his first twenty years.

It wasn't about money—to his father, maybe, but not to him. It was about standing by the only family he had in this world, even if he couldn't be sure his father would do the same for him. Every time an opportunity like this came around, a chance to show his father he was worth something, a chance to make the distant man proud, he'd felt the need to seize it, for fear of what would happen if he didn't.

He had tried to be honest about it, tried to be sincere. Since joining his father's company, he'd focused on doing the best he could, winning accounts, and proving himself to his father. He sacrificed a personal life; the only people he needed were his family, even if they were always barely out of reach. And then Lila had to come into his life, and remind him of what he was missing. Reminded him of another time in his life. A time he'd tried to forget.

He could still remember the way he felt when his father targeted Lila. The icy wash that had flooded his chest. He could still see the scorn in his father's eyes when Sam asked him to give her one more chance. Preston saw it as a weakness, telling him the only way he could really get ahead was to surround himself with equally strong people. People who would get you where you needed to be, not hold you back.

And look where my decisions have gotten me, Sam thought. He was alone, and the only person in this world who really knew him, really cared about him, might end up hating him forever.

The cab driver glanced at the rearview mirror and caught Sam's eye. "At the corner?"

Sam looked out the window at the rows of brick apartment buildings and nodded stiffly. "Right here, actually."

He paid the fare quickly and opened the door. It was a humid day and his shirt clung to his back, reminding him of all those long summer evenings he'd spent here with his grandmother. She'd sip lemonade and chat with the neighbors, while he rode his secondhand bike on the sidewalk, sometimes all the way down to the corner store to get a Popsicle from the freezer. He could still remember the merriment in her kind blue eyes when she took a wet dish towel and wiped his face clean, clucking her tongue in mock sternness.

The street felt different, somehow. The trees felt bigger. The apartment building, smaller. He hadn't been back to this neighborhood since his grandmother had died; when the only family he knew was gone, and an entire family he didn't know was still out there somewhere.

He'd been lonely. Lonely and scared and determined. He'd thrown himself into his studies, into bettering his life. There were no fallbacks. No home to return to anymore. When the other kids in his dorm went home for the holidays, Sam stayed behind. When summer break came along, he found part-time work and temporary roommates. He researched Preston Crawford, poring over the details he discovered, trying to form a complete picture of this man. His father. He had to know. He had to find out more. He knew he wouldn't stop until he did.

Sam shoved his hands in his pockets and walked down the street, making a loop around the block. He recognized a building where his best childhood friend had lived and frowned, wondering what had happened to the guy. Maybe he was married, maybe he had kids. Maybe his parents still lived in the cozy two-bedroom apartment that Rex would no doubt scoff at. Up ahead was the playground—he used to spend hours on those monkey bars, trying to beat his best time across to the other side. Children were shouting and squealing, running up the stairs and pushing their way down the slide. Sam settled on a bench under a maple tree and watched them play, just as his grandmother had all those years ago.

He hadn't forgotten a thing. Not one damn thing. Not the way he'd cried for a father when all the other kids at school bragged about going to ball games with their dads, not the way he had looked at himself in the mirror and wondered why his own father didn't want him, why he was worthless. And not the way his grandmother had brushed away his tears and set him straight, and told him that Preston Crawford didn't deserve him, and that Sam was better off not knowing him at all.

Sam stood and rolled back on his heels. Maybe he would have been. Or maybe it was better to know, to give it his all, and to admit defeat.

After a while, Sam walked a few blocks to a busy intersection and hailed a cab. He stared silently out the window as it transported him back to Manhattan—the whole other world he'd built for himself.

The doorman greeted him in the lobby and pressed the elevator button for him. Sam stepped inside the cool, air-conditioned box, letting the sweat roll off his body until a chill coated his skin. His apartment was the only one on the floor, and when the door slid open he walked into the living room, the vast empty space, the wall of windows with a view of Central Park and the buildings behind it, and somewhere far beyond, the place where he'd grown up.

And the place he'd left behind.

Chapter Thirteen

The Chicago skyline sat in the distance against a bright blue backdrop. Not a cloud was in the sky. Sam sank back against the leather headrest of the limo, watching as the buildings grew closer and wishing he could run in the opposite direction. There had been a steady breeze when they'd come out of the airport; it was perfect boating weather. Only there wouldn't be a date with Lila on the lake today. And there might never be one again.

"Is the freelance copywriter going to be there?" Rex asked. The brothers had spent most of the plane ride in tense silence, and Sam sadly admitted to himself they had little in common outside the business and their desire to earn their father's respect.

Sam shifted his gaze to Rex, who was leaning against the opposite car window, staring at him expectantly for an answer. "I don't know," he said, thinking of the calls he hadn't returned and hating himself for it. He hadn't been able to bring himself to listen to the messages Lila had left either. He was afraid. Afraid that the sound of her voice would make him lose his nerve. Afraid of what would happen if the one thing he'd lived for was finally gone. Twelve years of his life had gone into becoming his father's son. If he wasn't that, then what was he?

A coward, he thought, scowling. "I didn't invite her, but Reed Sugar might have."

"Guess it doesn't matter," Rex said with a shrug, and Sam said nothing. It hadn't occurred to him until now that Lila might be there, that he'd have to see the question in her eyes, see the look on her face when she saw him walk in with Rex. She'd assume the worst of him. She'd think he'd gone behind her back. And hadn't he, in a way?

"We're almost there," Sam said, as the driver moved into the right lane.

"Let's make this quick and easy, Sam," Rex warned. "If they want our business, they have to play by our rules."

Sam shifted his gaze to the back of the driver's seat, unable to even look his brother in the eye. "I can handle this. I don't even know why you insisted on coming," he added.

"To show them we mean business," Rex said. "And to make sure you don't waver on account of that girl."

"Give me some credit," Sam snapped, his eyes blazing as he glared at his brother, thinking back on what he'd done, the choice he'd already made, the look in Lila's eyes when she'd walked out of the agency that terrible day. There had been one mission in his life—one—and yet even now, after everything, it was still just out of reach.

Rex's phone pinged and he glanced at the screen, momentarily distracted. Sam set his hands on his briefcase, contemplating its contents, the presentation that was built on Lila's ideas. They were exiting the highway now. There wasn't much time left.

"I'd still like to know how the hell they found out about Jolt Coffee," Rex mused.

"It doesn't matter," Sam replied. Dread was building as quickly as their drive was ending. They'd be there any minute. "The bottom line is they know, and soon everyone else will, too."

"Well, that's cynical of you, Sam."

Something suddenly clicked. "Jolt Coffee is one of Reed's clients. They supply the sugar packets."

A slow, wry smile curved Rex's mouth. "Jesus. You're right."

Sam shifted in his seat and leveled his brother with a hard look. "Tell me, Rex, do you care about anything, and I mean *anything*, other than this damn company?"

"Hey, that's my family's company you're talking about," Rex hissed. "It's a part of me in a way you could never understand."

Sam stared at his brother, unable to say anything. His chest rose and fell with each breath, and his heart was beginning to pound with awareness. The agency was their father's baby—his first love. Maybe his only love. And Rex was just as desperate to compete with it as Sam was. But there was no rising above it, and no winning.

He felt sad for his brother. But he could only feel angry with himself. He was the lucky one, after all. For eighteen years, he'd known something better.

The driver swerved to a stop at the curb. Sam peered out the window for any sign of Lila inside, but the dark interior of the restaurant proved his effort impossible.

Rex paid the driver and reached for the door handle. "Ready?"

Sam didn't move. It was now or never. He'd been given a second chance in life. With a family. And with Lila. What happened today would change everything.

"I have a stop to make before the meeting," Sam said. His voice was tight with nerves, of the realization of what he was setting in motion.

Rex checked his watch. "Our meeting is in an hour!"

"This won't take long," Sam replied.

Rex's jaw pulsed, but he released the latch. "Don't mess this up, Sam," he said, as he climbed out of the car and slammed the door shut.

Sam let out a breath he hadn't even known he'd been holding.

Oh, I don't intend to, he thought.

*

Lila pulled open the door to the café, closed her eyes,

and took a good long breath. She loved the smell of freshly ground coffee, and today she loved it a little more than usual. She was depending on it, after all, to get her through what was panning out to be a very long Monday.

"What'll it be today?" Hailey grinned from behind the counter. "A croissant?" Lila's standard order if she went beyond a regular drip. "A lemon bar?" A summer treat.

"An extra large cappuccino and a double fudge brownie," Lila replied.

Hailey's smile immediately slipped. No good news ever called for that brownie. "Uh-oh. What happened?"

Lila hesitated, and then thought, *What the heck?* There was little point in being an independent contractor if you couldn't roll in a little late sometimes, and besides, she could use a friend right now. Anything beat sitting in that office, working on the Reed account, and wondering what on earth was going on with it.

The more time that ticked by without a call from Sam, the more suspicious she was becoming. And paranoia didn't sit well with her. It made her stomach hurt, and it left circles under her eyes that no amount of cold compresses could fix.

Hailey prepared the drink and handed her a mug. Lila took a sip. Ah. Now this would do the trick.

She paid for the items and took them over to the counter, where she could chat with Hailey near the espresso machine. The device hissed and steamed and the smell alone could perk her up. Already the day felt a little brighter.

But only a little.

"Okay, what did he do?" Hailey asked.

"How'd you know it was a he?"

Hailey lifted an eyebrow. "Isn't it always?"

Lila laughed. Sadly, it usually was. "Okay, yes, there is a guy, but it's not the kind of trouble you think." Well, it was, but Lila didn't feel like getting into the way her heart felt like it was being twisted and pulled in every possible direction, and the only reason she felt justified in eating what was probably a one-thousand-calorie dessert for breakfast was because she'd been unable to keep anything down yesterday. She was lovesick. She knew all the signs. She'd experienced them before . . . the last time Sam broke her heart.

"Go on," Hailey nudged. She poured some milk into a stainless steel cup and began frothing it.

Lila watched her work for a moment, thinking of where to even begin, when her phone rang. Her heart jumped, and she tipped over the tall mug, spilling the hot drink all over the counter and, unfortunately, the delicious brownie.

Hailey dropped a rag on the table. "Don't worry about it. You just answer your phone. Something tells me it might be him."

Lila hated the surge of hope that had crept into her chest. Something told her it might just be Sam, too.

She fumbled to get the phone out of her bag, her mind racing with everything she would say when she finally got her chance. If he thought she was going to make this easy for him, he had another thing coming. He'd have to have a damn good excuse to make up for this one.

But as much as she was furious, a bigger part of her was relieved. He was calling. They'd talk about Reed. Everything might be okay. After all, the meeting was still two days away.

Lila pulled the device free and turned it over to connect the call, but her breath caught when she saw the name on the screen. Jeremy Reed. This couldn't be good.

She tapped a button and pressed the phone to her ear. "Hello?"

"Lila, it's Jeremy. Listen, I wanted to let you know my first appointment ran long and we're running a little late."

Lila frowned. "Excuse me?"

"We'll probably be there by quarter after. Sorry about this."

Lila gripped the phone tighter. Her heart was doing jumping jacks. "Jeremy, I'm sorry, I—I don't know what you're talking about."

"The meeting? This morning? Sam pushed the date up." In the background, another man's voice could be heard. Mitch Reed. They were all together. All prepped and ready, while she . . .

Lila blinked. The room around her had gone dark, the voice on the other end of the phone, gone. The blood was rushing in her ears, making her mind spin and her fingers tremble.

"Lila? Did I lose you?"

"I'm still here, Jeremy," she managed. She chewed her bottom lip, knowing she had to think fast. So he'd done it. He'd gone behind her back and set something up, deliberately choosing to cut her out of the deal, even when he knew what she stood to lose, how important her family's business was to her. She'd let him into her world, into the part of her soul she had shielded him from all these years.

And he didn't care. Not about her. Not about Mary. Not about Sunshine Creamery.

She winced when she thought of her sister and how crushed she looked when they talked about selling the parlor.

Mary deserved more. This was Lila's moment to make that happen.

She let out a slow breath. She couldn't get emotional now. Not with so much at stake.

She had learned from Sam, and in that way, she had learned from the best. She would go the meeting with Reed, and so help her, she would land that account. With or without Sam Crawford.

*

Lila set her phone back in her bag and stood. She had to hurry. She had to get back to the office and make some notes, then she had to flag down a cab to take her downtown. Did she even have enough cash on her? Oh, and this outfit! She'd worn a sundress today, taking into account only the morning forecast and not the possibility of a meeting.

It would have to do. She had no choice. Sam hadn't left her with one.

"Bad news?" Hailey looked worried as she handed Lila another cappuccino. This one in a lidded paper cup.

"You could say that again," Lila muttered. "Thanks for this. I'm gonna need it."

"But you never told me what happened with that guy!" Hailey called after her as Lila wove her way through the people lining up for their morning caffeine fix.

Lila pushed open the door and looked back at her friend. "Let's just say there's nothing to tell," she said, because there wasn't. Everything that had happened last week had been an illusion. And now, it was time to face reality.

Lila scurried down the sidewalk, her bag in one hand, her drink in the other, trying not to slosh the beverage as she hurried up the steps of the brownstone of her office. Jim Watson was just getting in, too. He was often late on Mondays; sometimes he'd poke his head in, ask the girls about their weekend, but as Lila rushed passed him, he simply stood back to let her pass. Lila flashed him a smile of gratitude. It was nice to know there were still some nice men in the world.

"Was that Jim I saw coming in just now?" Penny asked as Lila hurried into her office.

She flicked on the light and turned on her laptop.

"Yep."

"Oh." Penny stood and came closer to her office. "That looked like a new shirt he was wearing. I don't think I've ever seen it before."

Lila glanced up from the computer screen. Penny was standing in the doorway, but her neck was craned as she stared at the front door, even though it was closed. Her blond bob was pulled back in a headband, and there was a telltale smudge of lipstick on her mouth. A new shade, Lila observed.

The laptop had finished powering up, and Lila quickly clicked on the folder where she kept all her notes pertaining to Reed. She'd planned to share all this with Sam, but now she'd take it directly to the client. Some of the ideas were nothing more than half-formed bullet points, but it would have to be enough. She'd talk through it. She was good on her feet. When she needed to be.

And she needed to be her best today. Now more than ever.

"Jim and I ended up on the same 'L' train the other night," Penny was saying.

Lila looked up distractedly, unsure of what to say. "That's nice. Does he live near you?"

"It turns out he does." Penny blushed. "We talked a bit. He's a nice man. I never noticed how green his eyes are."

Despite her stress, Lila grinned. "He does have beautiful eyes," she said with a wink.

The phone at the front desk rang and Penny left to answer it, seeming considerably lighter in her step than she had been just a few days ago. It was funny how love could do that to you, Lila mused. It could lift you up in the most surprising ways.

And it could crash you down when you least expected it.

She gritted her teeth and pulled the notes from the printer, then stuffed them into a folder. She glanced at the cuckoo clock. She'd have to leave soon. Quickly, Lila pulled out her wallet and thumbed through the cash. It would be enough to get her to the restaurant where the meeting was being held. At least that much was under control.

She froze and set a hand on the desk, allowing herself a moment to gather her thoughts. She didn't know what she would say to Sam when she saw him. How she could even look him in the eye after this kind of betrayal. When she thought of what he'd done. The chain of events that had led to this. The deliberate deception.

Tears prickled the back of her eyes, and she fanned them away. There wasn't time to cry now. She'd cry later, after she won the account. And so help her, she would win that account.

Sam may have ruined her hope for a second chance for them, but he wasn't going to take a second chance away from Sunshine Creamery.

Grabbing the papers, Lila stuffed them into a folder

and grabbed her bag. "Meeting," she explained to Penny as she hurried back to the front door. She reached for the handle, but the door pushed open before she could turn the knob. She stepped back with growing impatience, desperate to be on her way, to be the first party there, with any luck, to beat Sam at his own game.

The door creaked, inching open, forcing Lila's attention. She felt the color leave her face as a man appeared in the frame.

It was Sam.

Chapter Fourteen

"What the hell are you doing here?" Lila demanded, blocking his path into the waiting room of her office. She raked her eyes over him, noting the suit, the tie, and felt her anger boil to the surface. He was ready for the big meeting with Reed, while she was left in a pink sundress and flip-flops and a folder full of haphazard scribbles.

Sam didn't flinch. He didn't smile. He didn't even blink. He just stared at her with those piercing blue eyes and that little pinch between his brows that made her have a way of doubting herself. She stood a little straighter, recalling his silence, the numerous phone calls that had gone ignored. The meeting he'd rescheduled with Reed. Behind her back.

"I have to be somewhere," Lila said, pushing past him into the vestibule. She stopped and nailed him with a hard look. "And according to Jeremy Reed, you do, too."

His eyes flickered, but that was all he gave away. "Lila, five minutes, please."

Lila stared at him heavily, hedging her position. There was only one thing he could say right now that could take it all back, and he wasn't going to say it. He couldn't say it. He didn't have it in him.

Sam wasn't a man who lived by his heart. Sam didn't even have a heart. She of all people should know that by now. For someone who wanted so desperately to be accepted by their father, he'd done a mighty fine job of proving he was a Crawford.

"Sorry, Sam. I've wasted enough time on you." The words were out, clear and crisp in delivery. She could do this—she had to. She couldn't let her guard down again. Not with Sam.

Fool me once . . . Shame on her for daring to open her heart to him a second time. She'd be damned if she did it a third.

Over his shoulder she caught Penny's wide-eyed stare. Her mouth had formed a little circle. If there was a bowl of popcorn in reach, no doubt she'd be dipping her hand, taking in the show.

Releasing a sigh of frustration, Lila turned and pushed out into the warm morning sun. Below her on the street, shops were opening for the day, owners were turning signs and watering flowers, and people were strolling by with beach totes, enjoying the perfect summer day. She hurried down the stairs, wanting to join them, wanting to forget everything that was happening. Wanting to forget the way her heart was breaking . . . all over again.

"Lila, wait!"

She was already halfway down the stairs when she realized she should stop. Jeremy had said the meeting had been arranged by Sam, and yet here he was. If he had something to tell her before she hailed a cab, she wanted to hear it.

But it stopped there. All they had left was a professional tie. Not a personal one.

She looked up at him. "Five minutes," she said, folding her arms across her chest.

Sam walked down the stairs, holding his palms up in front of him. "I just want to explain. I just need you to hear me out."

Lila shifted on her feet. She glanced down the street. No sign of a cab.

Turning back to face him, she squared her jaw as her eyes met his. She wasn't going to let him get to her. Not now. Not after everything. "What about the meeting with Reed?"

Sam shrugged. "What about it?"

A fresh burst of fury coursed through her. "Don't play games, Sam. Jeremy called. I know you pushed up the meeting. Thanks for bothering to tell me."

"It was my brother, Lila. Rex called Mitch."

Lila stared at Sam in disbelief, and then barked out an unhappy laugh. "Of course. And good brother that you are, you stood back and let it happen and then didn't think to inform me."

Sam's expression looked pained. "Lila, I told you . . . when it comes to my family, it's complicated."

"And I told you, Sam, what landing this account meant to me. To my family. That ice cream parlor may not seem like much to you, but I can tell you, it's everything to my sister. And it was everything to my grandparents." She cursed under her breath as hot tears welled in her eyes. She didn't want him to see her like this. He didn't deserve to know how much he'd hurt her.

She could only imagine what Mary would say when she knew it was gone. That they'd have to sell the parlor, say good-bye to their grandparents all over again, and close the door on any family history they had left. Her sister was working two jobs to pull her weight, and it was such a simple thing to want. She wasn't going to get rich. Or famous. All she wanted was to make ice cream, to work hard, and to put a smile on everyone's faces. The way Gramps had.

Lila swallowed the lump that had formed in her throat.

"Lila." Sam took a step toward her, but she backed up until she was standing on the sidewalk. "I know how much that place means to you."

"No." She crossed her arms tightly over her chest, and shook her head forcefully. "You can't. That ice cream parlor is all I have left of my grandparents . . . of my mother. All my sister and I have left of them is Sunshine Creamery. And you took away the only chance I had to hold onto it. All to what? Make your father proud by showing you're just as ruthless as he is? That's a pretty sad way of impressing someone, if you ask me."

He reached the sidewalk, his gaze travelling to the shops across the street, and finally back to her. He rubbed a hand over his jaw, seeming to contemplate something, and then met her square in the eye. "Lila, I didn't leave the other day because of business."

"Oh no?" A part of her was interested, but the other part of her said not to bother listening to his sorry excuse. Time was ticking by, and unless he had something to tell her about the meeting, she couldn't afford to let him make her late for it.

She scowled. This was probably all part of the plan. Rex probably sent him over here to stop her from making a scene. To stall her from making an appearance at all. The Crawfords stopped at nothing to get what they wanted. How could she have overlooked that?

"My father didn't retire from PC Advertising," Sam said with a huff.

Lila pursed her lips. When she'd heard he'd left his sons to take over the company, she'd been perplexed. Preston Crawford was only in his sixties, and that agency was his life.

"My father has Alzheimer's," Sam said. "He's a proud man, and that agency means everything to him. He stepped down on his own, but it was still against his will."

Lila stopped looking for a cab and glanced at him. His

forehead was creased. His mouth was pulled into a thin line. And the little part of her that had loved him, and had listened to him open up to her the other night, couldn't turn her back on him now.

"Sam." Lila blinked, trying to understand what he was telling her. "I'm sorry. I had no idea."

"No one has any idea," Sam replied, his eyes hard. "Well, not many. My father's a proud man. Too proud, if you ask me."

"So that's why you went back." Shame tore at her when she considered how hard on him she'd been. If he could have just been honest . . .

She stopped herself. Sam had never been very forthcoming.

Sam nodded. "Yes. He had a setback. It was worse than the last time, and . . . I wouldn't have felt right if I didn't go see him. Even if he probably didn't care if I was there."

Her heart broke for him, but despite it, she couldn't overlook the phone calls that had gone ignored. The meeting that had been set up without her knowledge. Preston said jump, and Sam jumped. And in this case, Lila could only assume that Preston had ordered her off the account. They had her ideas now, so what purpose could she serve?

"And everything else?" she asked.

"I didn't plan it, Lila. It just happened." Sam set his jaw. "We're about to lose a major client. Gaining a new one seemed like the best way to save face."

"And sharing the credit with a freelance copywriter you fired six years ago stood in the way," Lila concluded.

Sam's eyes drooped. "It wasn't like that, Lila. I tried to tell—"

"You tried. Just like you tried to stop your father from letting me go all those years ago." Lila knew he could see the hurt in her eyes, but she didn't even care now. "It's one thing if I deserved to be let go. But I didn't, Sam. I know it, and I think you know it. I didn't deserve it. I don't deserve any of this."

"I loved you, Lila," Sam said quietly. "I think you're the only girl I've ever loved. You saw me for who I really am."

"Oh, you can bet on that." Her laugh was brittle. She looked away, before the tears fell again.

"You saw the real me. Not the person I've tried to be." Sam took another step toward her and grabbed her arm before she could back away. "I don't want to be that person anymore, Lila. I don't want to be Sam Crawford."

"But your father. Your brother. That agency!"

"Screw the agency," Sam spat.

Lila gasped in surprise. "But—" Her mind whirred. The meeting. Reed Sugar. What was he saying?

"I'm done with it, Lila. I don't . . . I don't like the person it's made me become. I've tried so hard to get to know my father, to make him proud, to make him want me in his life. And now, well, I've realized that's never going to happen." Seeing her expression, he added, "Not because of his illness, but because I don't think anything I could ever do would make him truly love me. He is who he is. I wanted to know him, and now I do. It's time to let go of the fight."

Lila shook her head, trying to imagine how it must feel to love someone who could never return the sentiment. He'd given up everything for one person. Including her. "I'm sorry, Sam."

"Not as sorry as I am," Sam said. "I wasted too many years. Years I can never take back."

She was crying now, crying for the sadness she saw in Sam's eyes, for the dream that had come crashing down around her, for the loss of Sunshine Creamery, and for the heartbreak Mary was about to experience all over again. She'd fallen for Sam. Long and hard and fast, and it had cost her everything. "Sam—"

He put a finger to her lips. "I lost you once before. I can't bear the thought of losing you again. Six years ago I made a choice. Now I'm making another one."

*

A cab came down the street and Sam lifted his arm swiftly, holding it high until the car swerved to a stop. They had to hurry if they were going to get to the restaurant before the Reed team arrived. There was no telling what damage would be done if Rex got to them first.

"Get in," he told Lila firmly.

"What?" Her brows creased in confusion. She didn't

move, even as he opened the car door.

Sam waved her over, more forcefully this time. "Get in. We're going to be late for the meeting."

Lila looked at him in despair. "What are you talking about, Sam?"

"I'm talking about the meeting." He waited a beat, but she remained firmly in place, a solid five feet from the curb. "Lila, I told you. I made a choice. And I chose you. You earned this account, and so help me, you're going to get it. Now, do you want to hand over Reed Sugar to Rex, or do you want to get in this cab with me and win the business?"

Lila blinked and then hurried across the sidewalk. He grabbed her elbow and helped her into the backseat as he rattled off the address of the restaurant where his brother was already waiting. He glanced at Lila, hating what he saw. He'd thought she'd be happy, he'd thought she'd forgive him, but instead she just stared out the window, biting her thumbnail, blinking rapidly.

"I'm not ready," she announced. "I didn't have time to prepare anything."

"Maybe not," Sam said, "but I did."

Lila's eyes widened in surprise. "You?"

Sam grinned. He nodded and pulled a folder out of his briefcase. He showed her a few visuals, rough sketches of a potential ad. Two little girls sharing an ice cream cone on a park bench. A dog at their feet licking a cone that had fallen.

"Oh, Sam." Her voice cracked on his name, and he reached over and squeezed her hand. "That dog. It reminds me of the painting at Sunshine Creamery."

"That's where I got the idea," Sam said. "Do you like it?"

"Like it?" Lila laughed. "I love it. But . . . I still don't understand. You didn't call—"

Sam closed the folder. He could only imagine Rex's expression when he walked into the restaurant with Lila, and his gut burned with fresh anxiety at the underhanded tactic. It wasn't in his nature to do something like that—it was in Rex's nature. Preston's nature. Maybe his brother was just taking the lead. Or maybe his brother was no different than him—desperate to please a man who could never be satisfied.

He checked his watch. If they made good time, they'd arrive before Reed. He'd talk to his brother. Tell him that he was walking away from the agency. But that he hoped he wasn't walking away from his family.

It was up to them now. They could take him as he was. He was ready for the risk.

"I had to figure things out, Lila. I had to be sure." And now he was. He'd given years to that family, trying desperately to belong, willing to do anything it took to prove he was one of them, even if it meant becoming like them. He was exhausted. Defeated. And for the first time since he'd knocked on the door of that stone mansion, walked through the cool dark halls, and shook the hand of the man with the ice blue eyes, he felt like he could breathe again. There was nothing to hide. Nothing to pretend. He didn't have to try anymore.

Lila's eyes searched his face, her expression seemed torn, as if she wanted to believe him, but didn't know how. And how could he blame her?

"And are you sure?" she asked.

He smiled. "It was always you, Lila. Even when I didn't want it to be, even when I told myself it wouldn't work. I tried to forget you, but I never did. This was our second chance, Lila. We can still have it, if you want it."

A tear fell from the corner of Lila's eye, and Sam brushed it off her cheek with the pad of his thumb. "We've wasted a lot of time, Sam."

"And I don't intend to lose another second," he said as he leaned in to kiss her.

Epilogue

The line for Sunshine Creamery extended out the door and down the block, but no one thought to turn back or try something else. Children clung to their parents' hands, waiting patiently for a taste of Mary's most popular creation, the quadruple scoop, triple dip waffle cone.

"Only Mary," Lila laughed, as she and Sam joined the line. "I can only imagine what my grandparents would say if they could see this."

"Personally, I like the bucket list sundae. Why choose just one when you can have a scoop of all forty flavors?" He flashed a wicked grin, and Lila could only shake her head.

Since Sunshine Creamery had officially reopened at the beginning of August, she and Sam often stopped by to visit Mary on the weekends, sometimes even rolling up their sleeves to help with the effort if the crowds got too big.

It had been a busy July, with all three of them brainstorming late into the night about branding and marketing. Lila helped Mary with a website, and Sam came up with a tagline for the flyers she posted around the city. They spent nearly every weekend rolling fresh paint, scouting for new tables and chairs, and taste testing the menu—Sam's favorite part, Lila couldn't help but notice.

"I still can't believe you ordered that thing," she said, recalling the stares from other patrons when Mary happily set the platter of ice cream on their table last Friday night, right after their sushi dinner.

"Hey, I'm a fan of supporting local businesses," Sam said. "Besides, our biggest client supplies one of the main ingredients. How could I resist?"

"Oh, so that's your excuse then? Showing your allegiance to Reed Sugar by indulging in enough ice cream to feed a little league team? Maybe our next client should be a dentist."

"You know, that's not a bad idea, Lila. But then, that's why I went into business with you." Sam winked, and Lila reached down to take his hand.

She'd had reservations when Sam suggested they team up, but only for a few minutes—he had a way of winning her over like that. Sure, Sam was stubborn, and he might not always agree with her brilliant ideas, but he had plenty of his own, and together, they were better than they were alone.

In every possible way, she thought, adjusting her hand so her fingers laced with his.

Finally they neared the front of the line, where Mary had set up some small bistro tables and white benches. Planters bursting with brightly colored flowers flanked the open door, just below the crisp pink-striped awning that had replaced the old, faded one. The sign was the only thing that hadn't changed, because some things never did, and, Lila thought with a little tug in her heart, never should.

"Oh, look, Penny and Jim are here," Lila said as they stepped into the air-conditioned room. The cool air prickled her clammy skin. It had been a hot, sticky day, and she was looking forward to another day on the lake tomorrow with Sam. He was determined to make a sailor out of her, and she wasn't going to argue with that.

"They seem to be getting along well these days," Sam observed.

When they'd decided to go into business together, they'd had no choice but to upsize their office space. The panic that had rolled through Penny's expression confirmed Lila's suspicions about her feelings for Jim, until Lila happily announced they were relocating just upstairs, directly next to Jim's office. Soon Jim started casually popping in to see if Penny was closing up for the day, and the two could be seen walking to the "L" stop together, as cute as two high school sweethearts.

Lila waved to her assistant and their office neighbor. "How funny to see them here," she observed, even though she knew they were loyal patrons, like so many other special people in her life. Hailey had even hung up a sign on the bulletin board in her café and handed her customers coupons for free scoops during their opening week.

"Isn't that Hailey over there, too?" Sam tapped her on the shoulder and motioned to the corner where Hailey sat with a banana split and a hundred-watt smile.

Lila waved again. "What a bizarre coincidence," she murmured.

Behind the counter, Mary cleared her throat. "What will it be today?" she asked. Her eyes gleamed, as they did every day since the parlor had reopened.

"I'll have the Sunshine sundae," Lila said.

"No triple dip cone?" Sam lifted a brow, trying not to laugh.

"What can I say? I'm old-fashioned." Lila winked.

"Make that two Sunshine sundaes," Sam added. Glancing at Lila, he said, "Believe it or not, I'm a man of tradition myself."

Lila swatted his arm and went to find a table. She would have liked to have stopped to chat with Hailey, but she was on the phone now, and besides, she'd chosen a small table with only one chair. Jim and Penny were too busy gazing into each other's eyes to even notice her as Lila crossed the room, managing to scout out a pedestal table near the window.

She settled into her chair, watching with amusement as Sam walked over to the jukebox and selected a song. She'd expected something old-timey or upbeat, but for some reason he chose a slow tune, one she couldn't really name, but somehow knew.

"Do you know this one?" he asked, coming to sit across from her. His blue eyes danced, and something told her he was up to something. "It was playing the night of our first date."

Lila blinked. She had thought she was the only one who remembered their first date at a little diner just a few blocks from the office. He'd suggested dinner, and she'd agreed, not thinking it would be anything more than a friendly evening, but wishing with all her heart that it could be. They'd laughed and talked and at the end of the night he'd kissed her. Right there on the sidewalk, with the wind rustling through the leaves.

She was wearing a black wool coat and a red scarf that matched her lipstick. He was wearing a blue shirt and a silk tie. She could still remember that tie.

She'd thought she remembered every detail. The way she'd fiddled nervously with her earrings. The way Sam suggested they split a dessert. The way his eyes crinkled at the corners when he smiled at her. The way her heart beat a little faster every time he did.

"There was a jukebox on the table," she mused, remembering now. She squinted at him. "You remember the song?"

"Honey, I remember everything." Sam winked.

Mary arrived at the table then, a large sundae in each hand. Lila smiled at the little sun-shaped shortbread cookie tucked into the side of the dish—Mary had come up with that idea, too. It was their grandmother's recipe.

Lila picked up her spoon and dipped it thoughtfully into her ice cream. "You know, it's funny, but tonight, more than usual, I feel like I'm really home."

Sam sat across from her, watching her carefully. She noticed he hadn't reached for his spoon yet.

She narrowed her eyes. Suspicious.

"A few months ago, I felt like everything was gone, and now . . . We're all here. You. Me. My sister. Hailey. Jim and Penny." She smiled at the cookie. "I feel like my grandparents are still here, too."

She blinked away the tears that prickled the back of her eyes. This was ridiculous, getting emotional like this, on a warm summer Saturday evening, over a bowl of ice cream, for Pete's sake. She smiled away the emotions and reached down for the cookie, and that's when she saw it. There, wedged between a scoop of blueberry cheesecake (with chunks of graham cracker crust) and vanilla bean, was the sparkle of a diamond.

Lila gasped and glanced up at Sam, who was grinning ear to ear. The tears that had been building began to fall steadily now, and she didn't even try to stop them. Sam pushed his chair back and came around the small table to get down on one knee, and that's when Lila saw them—

her friends, her sister, standing behind him, clutching their hands, sharing in this moment.

And there, just over Mary's shoulder, was Gramps, captured in a framed print, watching it all . . .

Coming Soon

SWEETER THAN SUNSHINE

Mary Harris has always looked on the bright side…until one too many setbacks leave her wondering why she sacrificed everything for a failing ice cream parlor. Hopelessly single, and still licking her wounds from her last break-up, she almost manages to believe that she doesn't need a man when she has Sunshine Creamery, until the handsome guy next door has her second guessing herself, and her family's business.

Ben Sullivan's life was going exactly to plan—and he's been picking up the pieces ever since it all blew up. Now a single dad, he's determined not to let another woman mess with his heart again—or his daughter's. He tells himself he's only being neighborly by helping Mary repair some things in her shop, but the more time they spend together, the more he dares to wish for something he hasn't even thought about in a long time: a future.

Chapter One

Pretty as a postcard.

As much as she wished to deny it, Grace Madison knew that nothing could top Vermont at Christmastime. Drawing to a stop as the snow-dusted road rounded a bend, she stared at the bridge in the near distance, her lips pursed with displeasure. Snow was falling slow and steady, neatly covering the slanted roof in a white blanket. Someone had hung a wreath complete with a red velvet bow just above the arched opening, and icicles gave a natural picot edging to the red-hued truss.

With a sigh, Grace pressed on the accelerator and drove across the bridge, over the frozen water below, and into her childhood home of Briar Creek. The hand-painted sign to the side of the road welcomed her, boasting of a population the size of her city block in

Manhattan.

Make that her *old* city block in Manhattan, she corrected herself.

She continued down the familiar path, turning onto Mountain Road as the sun began to dip over the Green Mountains. Grace flicked on her windshield wipers and fumbled for her headlights, cursing herself for not having learned the way around her rental car when she'd first picked it up. She scrambled with the gadgets around the steering wheel, smiling in grim satisfaction when the warm yellow glow illuminated the vast stretch of road before her. It was times like this when she remembered why she truly did prefer city life. This was the first time she had driven a car in . . . well, longer than she should probably admit. She and Derek never kept a car in the city—when they needed to go somewhere, they just hailed a cab.

Derek. No need to think about him now. With thinning lips Grace reached over and snapped off the radio and the depressing reminders of its melodies, but as silence encroached and left her alone with her darkening thoughts she abruptly flipped it back on, desperate to find a station that wasn't bleating Christmas carols with limited interruption. Surely there must be a talk radio station somewhere. Something that wasn't a painful reminder of how lonely this Christmas was going to be for her.

Her windshield wipers were in overdrive, in a vain attempt to keep up with the swiftly falling flurries. Wind swirled the flakes, stirring them up from the road in front of her, blinding her path. She slowed her pace to a near crawl, wrapping her hands tighter around the steering wheel, and squinted through the pellets beating against the windshield.

Her tires skidded on a patch of ice, causing her heart to drop into her stomach, and she eased off the gas, fumbling for control until the car came to an abrupt stop.

Grace opened her eyes and looked around. She was staring at a wall of snow as high as the hood of her car. The woods around her were eerily quiet, and the only sound to be heard was the thumping of her own heart.

She swore under her breath. She not only had to figure a way to get the car on the road again but, unfortunately, she also still had to continue the drive. As if this trip wasn't bad enough already.

She checked herself quickly. She was not dead, or even injured, save the pinch mark on her arm where she managed to convince herself she really was still here. The impact had been comically soft, leading to nothing but complete aggravation about a trip that was already stressful enough. The ear- piercing scream she had released as the nose of the car collided with the snow pile had obviously been an overreaction— fortunately, no one was around to hear it. That also meant there was no one around to help, either.

The snow had turned heavy and wet, so that the flakes no longer flurried in the wind but instead created a dense blanket on the hood of the car. Gritting her teeth, Grace slid the transmission into reverse and gently pressed the gas pedal. When nothing happened, she gave it a little more force, wincing at the sound of her spinning tires. She clenched her hands around the steering wheel, feeling the panic squeeze her chest, and tried again. Nothing.

Without giving it any thought, Grace whipped off her seat belt and pushed open the car door. The wind howled around her, whipping her long, chestnut-brown hair across her face. The stretch of road before her was depressingly barren. The sun was starting to disappear over the mountains in the distance. It would be dark before long, and this old back road hadn't seen a plow all day. By nightfall, it wouldn't even be granted the light from a streetlamp.

Quickly, Grace walked to the front of the car, pressed her palms against the edge of the hood, and gave it a hard push, grunting at the effort. Four more attempts left her exhausted and upset. It was time to call for help. For not the first time today, she wished that Derek was here. This never would have happened if he had been driving.

Foolishness! She climbed back into the car, turning up the radio for company as she searched for her cell phone. It wasn't that she wanted Derek here—after all, they were over. Finished. She'd given back the ring; they had ended on good, if chilly, terms. No, she didn't want Derek here, not rationally speaking. She just wanted the things that Derek could provide, or at least, once had. Security, stability, safety. Comfort and joy. *Good tidings of comfort and*—Oh, that blasted Christmas carol!

Grace flicked off the radio and kept it that way. The last thing she needed right now was to get worked up. She had promised her mother she would arrive in time for dinner, and the last thing she owed anyone in her family was a frown by way of greeting. It would defeat the whole purpose of coming home at all.

She sighed again as she rummaged through her overstuffed handbag, still in search of her phone. Finding it buried beneath two candy bar wrappers and a receipt for the Christmas gifts tucked into her bags, she scrolled through the list of her family members until she found her youngest sister's number.

"Hello?" Jane's voice was barely audible above the clanking of pots. In the background, Grace could make out her mother's voice, followed by that of her middle sister, Anna. No doubt they were gathered in the warm, cozy kitchen right now, hovering around the big island that anchored the family home, squabbling over which side dish they should make, or who would cover the dessert. She imagined her little niece, Sophie, watching a classic holiday movie or making out her list for Santa.

Grace hesitated as she considered the gift she had bought Sophie for Christmas. She had no firsthand experience with four-year-olds, and Jane was forever raving about how quickly children changed. The last time Grace had seen her had been in the spring, and the time before that was when Sophie was only a year old when

Jane and Adam had visited New York for a long weekend. She had been startled by how different Sophie looked nine months ago, and reminded of how much she had missed by staying away all these years.

Well, all the more reason to chin up and make this Christmas count. It was time to start making up for lost time. Time to stop wallowing in her own sorrow.

"Hey there—"

"Where are you?" Jane hissed through the crackling connection.

Grace frowned. "What kind of greeting is that?" She considered turning the car around right then and there. She could be back in the city by midnight, tucked into her bed with a bowl of her favorite Thai delivery and one of those feel-good Christmas movies that they played by the dozen this time of year. But then she remembered that she wasn't exactly feeling the holiday cheer this year. And that she was stuck in a rental car on a snow embankment on one of Briar Creek's most remote roads. And that she no longer had her own bed or her own apartment to hide in. All of her possessions that weren't locked in a storage unit in Brooklyn, New York, were crammed into four bags in the trunk of this car. *Damn it.*

"Sorry," Jane said. "I didn't mean it like that. I'm just . . . stressed. You know how it is."

Yes, Grace did. This time of year always brought out a hyper, frenzied side to their mother, who would be fretting for weeks in advance over table arrangements and menus, who would stand twenty feet back from the porch and scrutinize the pine garland with narrowed concentration, until her three daughters would shiver with cold, finally rolling their eyes and retreating inside to the warmth of the fire while their father stood patiently awaiting her suggestions, adjusting the garland to her satisfaction with an amused twitch of his lips.

Kathleen Madison was hailed the "Christmas Queen" of Briar Creek. Their house won the Holiday House contest twelve years in a row, until Kathleen deemed it in poor taste to continue, graciously stepping aside to accept the role of judge. "Let's give another family a chance," she had whispered to the girls, suggesting that no one else in town even stood a chance so long as the Madisons were entered.

A freelance decorator, Kathleen saw Christmas as her biggest opportunity of the year. The interior of the Madison home was always finely detailed with a porcelain Christmas village in the bay window, and an antique train set looping around the spectacular Douglas fir that the family selected together each year at the tree farm. Twice the Madisons' tree had appeared on the front page of the *Briar Creek Gazette*. Their annual cards were each laboriously calligraphied by Kathleen's own hand, and she approached her holiday baking with the rigor typically reserved for army drills. Every neighbor, friend, and teacher looked forward to Kathleen's homemade gift basket; the annual Christmas bazaar relied on her to deliver. And she always did.

"Are you still coming?" Jane asked, trepidation dripping from her words.

"Of course I'm still coming!" Grace squinted through the falling snow, searching for a sign of headlights.

Seeing nothing, she fell back against the headrest, considering Jane's insinuation. She couldn't blame her sister for being skeptical. With the exception of that painful spring morning nine months ago, Grace had managed to stay clear of her hometown and the memories it held. Five years had passed since she'd first left home— not knowing at the time it would be for good—and each year that stretched successfully distanced her further from her past, until eventually her life was tied to New York, not the sleepy New England town. And definitely not to anyone in it.

"I told you I would be there by dinner," she added, furrowing her brow through the whiteout. She flicked her windshield wipers a notch higher. It was no use.

"I just wanted to be sure . . ." Jane trailed off as the connection began to crackle. "I didn't know if you had changed your mind at the last minute because of . . . well, you know."

"If you're referring to the person we shall not name, you have nothing to worry about. I've avoided him for years, and I plan to avoid him for the next week, too." Grace swallowed hard. It could be done. She'd stay at the house, reading books, baking cookies, and trying not to think about the proximity of her first love. Her first heartbreak. Or everything else she had lost recently.

"Besides, I'm not even sure why you're giving this any thought," she added with more conviction than she felt. "He and I are ancient history."

There was a pause on the other end of the line. "If you say so," Jane said softly.

Grace bit down on her lip, knowing it would be useless to try to defend herself. Jane knew her too well; Grace couldn't hide from her. Everyone in the family knew the reason why she had left Briar Creek and stayed away. It was all because of the man whose name they had promised never to say aloud in her presence. The man who could cause Grace's stomach to twist, her blood to still, and her heart to break all over again, just by mere mention.

She had changed her mind about this trip at least a dozen times, but in the end she knew there was no way around it. There was no telling what would prevail in Briar Creek while she was here. The wounds it would open. The scars it would sear. Her life was crumbling enough as it was— she couldn't risk any more upset.

Things were bleak. She'd managed not to think about it now for, oh—she checked the clock— seventeen minutes. Well, that was two minutes more than the last time she'd stumbled into her darkening thoughts. Her relationship wasn't the only thing that was over. Her career was rapidly unraveling as well.

She firmed her mouth. She couldn't think about any of this right now.

She slammed her foot on the accelerator, whimpering as the wheels ground deeper into the snow.

"Well, before you get here there's something I wanted to talk about—"

Grace almost managed to laugh. Now was hardly the time to settle in for a long chat. "Can we discuss this later, Jane? I'm sort of stuck in a snowbank here."

"What?" Jane's voice was shrill, and Grace pulled the phone away from her ear, bringing it back in time to hear her sister say, "Should I call the police?"

"Relax," she said, giving the pedal everything she had in her. "I'm fine. I just slid off the road and now I can't get this," she pressed on the gas once more, knowing it was pointless, but still hoping, "stupid car to move!"

"But you're okay?" came Jane's urgent reply, and Grace instantly regretted worrying her. With everything their family had been through in the past year, she knew all of them were feeling sensitive.

"Yes, I'm fine. We've been talking for minutes, haven't we?" Grace put the car in park and trained her eye on the rearview mirror. "I just . . . I need you to come and get me. I'm going to have to call for a tow." From the distance, Grace thought she detected the sudden glow of a car making its way through the darkness. She perked up, sitting straighter in her seat, watching intently as the headlights grow closer. Sure enough, the SUV slowed and then pulled to a stop in front of her. She bit back a smile as she began gathering her belongings, ready to make a swift getaway.

"Never mind, Jane," she said quickly. "Someone just pulled up."

"Oh, good," Jane gushed. "So you'll be here soon?"

"I'll hitch a ride into town, but I might need you to meet me there." She could wait in her father's bookstore if need be—the thought of it brightened her. There was one silver lining to coming back to Briar Creek, at least. Main Street Books always had a way of making her forget her troubles.

"Okay. If I don't hear from you, I'll assume you're on your way."

Grace disconnected the call, musing over their casual comfort at the mere notion of hitching a ride with a stranger. She would never consider such a thing elsewhere, if the opportunity was even granted. Things were different in these parts, though. If someone saw a car pulled over in Briar Creek, they'd stop and lend a hand. If the same situation happened in New York, they'd just keep on going.

A tapping at her window startled her and she quickly crammed empty coffee cups and evidence from an indulgent stop at a fast-food joint somewhere near the Vermont border into their bags. Smiling apologetically, she shifted to face the window, her breath locking in her chest when she saw Luke Hastings's equally shocked face peering back at her.

She stared at him, not blinking, clutching a grease-stained paper bag to her heaving chest. *This day keeps getting better and better.* She had barely skidded past the town line, and she was already running into the one man she had hoped to avoid. Forever.

The lights from his black Range Rover beamed strong, and Grace noticed with a heaviness in her heart that he hadn't lost his looks since she'd last seen him. If anything, his features had hardened into something more manly and strong. The fine lines around his dark blue eyes gave him character, and their deep-set intensity gave her the same rush it always had. *Damn him.*

Grace held his gaze, knowing she was trapped. She was at his mercy now. He could walk away, refuse to help, drive off and leave her stranded on this unlit mountain road. In a snowstorm. No man would do that, not even Luke. But oh, she bitterly wished he would.

For not the first time she found miserable irony in the fact that Luke was, and always had been, a gentleman.

Grace rolled down the window with the press of her finger. "What the hell are you doing here?" she demanded.

An inquisitive smirk passed over Luke's rugged features. "Shouldn't I be the one asking you that?"

"I'm here for Christmas," she said tightly.

"Christmas isn't for another week," he said gruffly.

"So, it's still my town."

He lifted an eyebrow. "Is it?"

Grace looked away. "You can be on your way, Luke. I just got off the phone with Jane; she can come and get me." Her face burned as she fumbled in her handbag for her cell phone, blindly reaching for wherever it had landed.

Luke assessed the situation with a frown. "Looks like you've gotten yourself into a bit of a jam." He studied her. "Are you hurt?"

Grace pinched her lips and shifted her gaze from his scrutiny, but her eyes kept flitting back. Despite the winter chill that nipped at her nose and fingers, she felt overheated and stifled. "I'm fine, thank you. Everything is just . . . fine." And it was, or it would be, when he left. When he turned his back and walked away, like he had all those years ago.

A hint of a smile passed over his lips. "Really."

"Yes, really!" With that, Grace raised the window, feeling a moment of relief for the thin glass that separated her from . . . from the man whose name was never to be mentioned. She knit her brow and turned to glare at the steering wheel. Clenching her teeth, she pulled the car into reverse and hit the accelerator at full throttle. The tires spun loudly, but the car didn't move.

Heart pounding, she stared despondently at the dashboard for a few seconds before shifting her eyes to Luke's penetrating gaze. The corner of his mouth twitched, those blue eyes sparked, and Grace dragged a deep sigh, digging her nails into her palms.

He pointed his finger toward the car handle, gesturing for her to unlock it. His intense stare fused with hers, hooded by the point of his brow. His full lips spread thin, giving insight into his displeasure.

Well, the feeling was mutual, Grace thought with a huff. Tearing her attention from him, she unlocked the door. An icy cold wind whipped her in the face as she pushed open the door.

"What were you doing driving on this road in these conditions?" Luke demanded as she climbed out of the car. His dark hair spilled over his forehead, slick with snow. "You should have taken Oak or South Main."

Grace yanked away his half-hearted gesture to help her, and he let his hand fall at his side. She narrowed her eyes at the smirk that curled at those irresistible lips. The lips she had known as well as her own. Every line, every curve, every taste. She squared her shoulders and met his eye stonily. "Well, I took Mountain Road, okay? Besides, I could say the same thing to you!"

Luke tipped his head. "Not really. I live off Mountain Road. And I have four-wheel drive."

Grace bristled. She hadn't even thought to take South Main, even though it would have been a straight shot into town. Somehow, subconsciously, she had driven herself in the direction of the one person she hoped to avoid. The little part of her that longed for something that could never be had overruled all rational thought. And now, well, she supposed she'd gotten what she'd wanted. She was standing here, staring into the face of the man she hadn't seen, with the exception of that one, fleeting time she'd rather forget, in five years.

"I meant driving in the snow. At . . . this hour." She motioned to the darkness all around them.

She watched as Luke fought off a smile. A sheen of amusement lit his eyes. He made a show of checking his watch. "It's five o'clock," he said. "And my place is just down that way, as you'll remember." The grin finally got the better of him.

"Well." Grace inhaled sharply, the cold air slicing her lungs, and looked away. The snow was coming down in heavy, thick flakes. The hood of her car had already collected at least an inch, and her hair felt wet and heavy against her gray wool coat. *Perfect snowman weather*, she couldn't help thinking. If she were feeling the Christmas spirit, that is—and she wasn't. She most certainly wasn't.

"What are you doing out here?" he asked.

"I told you. I'm on my way home."

His jaw hardened. "Thought you said you were never coming back to Briar Creek."

She glared at him. That was only half the story, and he knew it. "Jane asked me to come home," she explained. "With everything that's happened recently, I couldn't exactly say no."

Luke nodded slowly. "I suppose not." He looked to the ground, shoving his hands in his pockets. "I didn't know you were coming."

"That's a surprise. Word usually travels fast around here." She folded her arms across her chest defensively, eyeing him through the falling snow.

He narrowed his gaze. After a beat, he murmured, "Yes. Yes, it usually does."

With a sigh he broke her stare and wandered over to inspect the collision site. She waited to see if he would find amusement in her predicament, but he didn't seem to be in the mood for laughs. The realization disappointed her, all at once reminding her of what they once had and no longer did. Standing here with the one person who knew her best, alone in the dark, on this cold mountain road, she had never felt more alone.

"Well," Luke said, bending down to inspect the situation more closely. "It doesn't look like you're going to get it out of this bank on your own."

"I'll call for a tow truck then," she said, rummaging through her bag and inadvertently setting a candy bar wrapper loose. She watched it whip through the wind, somewhere in the direction of the woods, and she could practically see Luke chuckling from her periphery. Finding her phone, she furiously tapped the number for information and waited. Nothing. Her breath caught in her chest as she pulled the phone from her ear and glanced at the screen. Connection lost. Of course.

She eyed Luke furtively, feeling her anger burn as a twinkle of enjoyment flashed through his blue eyes. Was this so easy for him? Did he not feel anything?

"No connection?"

"I had one a minute ago . . ." She exhaled deeply, and then rolled back her shoulders to fix her gaze on him. A rumble of something dangerous passed through her stomach as she studied his face. Would he ever not have this effect on her? "If you don't mind going into town for a tow, I'll just wait inside the car." She paused, gritting her teeth as she hesitated on her next words. "Thank you."

He looked at her like she was half crazy. "You think I'm going to go for help and leave you out here?"

She shrugged. "Why not? You've done worse to me."

A flash of exasperation crossed his rugged features. He rubbed a hand over his tense jaw, his eyes sharp as steel. Grace knew that look, knew it all too well. She'd made him angry. *Well, good.*

"Get in my car," he ordered, jutting his chin in the direction of his big black vehicle. "It's freezing out here."

Grace tried to suppress the shiver that was building deep within her. She'd be damned if she let him see how cold she was in her simple wool peacoat. She planted her feet to the ground, but it was no use. She shuddered, then inwardly cursed as Luke's expression softened.

"Here, take my scarf." He started walking toward her, but she reflexively took a step back. He stopped, his shoulders slumping. "Grace. Take the scarf."

Grace lifted her chin, her lips thinning. She glanced at him out of the corner of her eye, and her heart panged. There he was. Her sweet love. Luke Hastings. The love of her life. The man who had chased her through the icy waters of the creek in the heat of summer. The man who had taken her to bed in cool, cotton sheets. The man who had kissed her until she wept, the man who had held her until she couldn't breathe. The man whose smile could warm her heart, and whose frown could stop it. The man who represented every part of her past, and who was supposed to have held every moment of her future. The man no one since had ever been able to live up to.

"Fine," she muttered, reaching out to take the navy scarf. As she tied it around her neck, she subtly breathed into the fabric, closing her eyes to familiarity of the musky scent. She fingered the fringe at the bottom, knowing she had never seen Luke wear this scarf in all the years they were together.

She wondered when he had gotten it. She wondered if his wife had bought it for him.

"Your bags in the trunk?" Luke asked, and Grace nodded. Without another word, he popped the trunk and pulled out two large bags. He carried them low at his sides to his car and then returned for the second round. "You never did pack light," he grumbled as he brushed past her.

Grace hung back as he loaded her belongings, and glanced despairingly at her rental car, which was obviously not going anywhere on its own. "Should have listened to my gut," she whispered to herself. *Shouldn't have come here at all.*

"You coming or not?" Luke called with obvious impatience.

Grace closed her eyes, shaking her head in the negative even as she began walking toward the glow of his taillights. Each crunch of snow under her boots brought her one step closer to the part of her she had tried to deny since the day she left this town for good. Each inch closer to Luke's world took her further out of the one she had built for herself.

She reached the passenger door and yanked it open. If she stepped inside this car—Luke's car—there would be no going back. She paused, her breath coming in ragged spurts. She wiped a strand of cold, wet hair from her forehead. Inside the car, Luke was watching her expectantly, the heat from the vents felt almost suffocating against the crisp evening air.

With one last breath for courage, she climbed inside and left the safety of her world behind with a slam of the door. Like it or not, she was back in Briar Creek. And so far, it was going even worse than expected.

Olivia Miles is a bestselling author of contemporary romance. A city girl with a fondness for small town charm, Olivia enjoys highlighting both ways of life in her stories. She currently resides just outside Chicago with her husband, daughter, and two ridiculously pampered pups.

Olivia loves connecting with readers. Please visit her website at www.OliviaMilesBooks.com to learn more.

Made in the USA
Middletown, DE
27 April 2018